Bring Me Sunshine

Wendy Storer

Published in 2013 by Applecore Books
www.applecorebooks.co.uk

Printed in Great Britain by Lightning Source
ISBN 978-0-9574812-8-2

For Alan

September Playlist

All the Small things
Blink 182: Travis Barker

Travis Barker will have to wait. I turn off my iPod to concentrate on finding Dad's wallet.

"I know I had it," says Dad. "I remember." He bangs the side of his head with his hand as if he's trying to knock the memory out. If only it was that easy. Dad's forgetfulness is, like, a daily event and I swear he can be the most infuriating person on the planet.

"Daisy," says Sam. "We've only got ten minutes."

"Plenty of time," I say, crossing my fingers because it's a lie.

Sam pokes his tongue out at me.

Ten minutes to find the wallet, get out of the house, buy some chips for tea and get across town, OR miss the start of the Torchlight Procession. But we can't go without cash so there's no choice.

"Okay, so if you remember having it, where were you at the time?" I say to Dad. "What were you doing with it?"

"I was dusting and…"

"You were what?"

Dusting + Dad = unbelievable.

"… and I made a cup of tea…" He frowns, and rolls his eyes upwards trying to recall. "Except the milk was off… so I was going to buy some more…"

"You went to the shops?" I say.

He looks into the distance and nods, slowly. "I think so."

I take a deep breath. "You can't remember if you went to the shops?" I say it in my patient voice, feeling more as if I am the mum talking to her kid, instead of the fifteen-year-old talking to her dad. But he's got what they call an artistic temperament, which means that he's always got his head in some creative fog and real life has to wait.

"Of course I can remember," says Dad. "It's just that I lose track... What did I do yesterday?"

I look at Sam. He's ready to go, wearing his beloved monkey hat with ears, sitting wonky on his head. It is way too small, but I'm not bothered.

"Help me look, will you?" I say to him. "We don't want to go without cash."

And then Dad says, "You're not letting him wear that are you?" - talking about the hat.

And Sam says, "I can wear what I want."

And Dad says, "If you want to look ridiculous."

"You're not even coming," says Sam, and then he storms out of the room and slams the door because he Hates, with a capital H, anyone telling him what to do. I wonder where he gets that from, Dad.

"Tell him to leave it here," says Dad, to me.

Honestly, I should work for the UN or something because I'm, like, family peace-keeper and chief negotiator all rolled into one. So I follow Sam into the kitchen and I've got no intention of laying down the law about hats; I just want him to help me find the wallet so we can escape for a couple of hours.

But as I open the door, Sam is there swigging milk straight from the carton. "Hey!" I shout. "What do you think you're...?"

But Sam's already spitting it back out. "Yeuch!"

Milky lumps land on the table. He wipes his tongue with his sleeve. "It's off!" he says. "See?" and shoves the carton under my nose.

"Oh take it away," I say. One whiff and it makes me retch. "Tip it down the sink."

Sam holds the carton upside down and we watch the lumps of milk drop onto the stainless steel, sperlatt sperlatt sperlatt, and slide towards the plug hole.

"Gross!" says Sam.

"That'll teach you." I turn the cold tap full on to wash the globs away.

"It's not me who needs teaching," Sam says. "I didn't leave it out. And it's not fair because he's allowed to do whatever he wants and no one tells him off, but ..."

"All right," I say. "So it wasn't you. But you still shouldn't drink from the carton. It's dirty." I don't know how many times I've told him that already. I pick up the dishcloth and some bleach spray, and clean milky spit from the table then rinse the carton and throw it in the bin. I look at the clock. "Just help me find Dad's wallet, please?" I offer him my hand for a high five and he slaps me hard, laughing.

When he looks happy with the amount of pain I pretend to be in, he starts looking; in the washing machine, the laundry basket and then the fridge. He's usually quite good at finding the things Dad loses, as if they're on the same mad wavelength or something, but I'm thinking he's way off the mark today. And I'm about to tell him to forget it, when he shouts, "Found it!"

Dad's wallet is inside the fridge door, on the milk shelf, nestled between a carton of juice and a can of Mr

Sheen. No milk. I raise my eyes, like, totally despairing, but Sam just thinks it's all very funny. I put the Mr Sheen under the sink with the other cleaning stuff, take a twenty pound note, and slip the wallet into Dad's coat pocket. We shout goodbye, and leave before he can have a go at anyone about the monkey hat.

You Can't Always Get What You Want
Rolling Stones: Jimmy Miller

There's a queue at the chippy.

"Can we get chips later?" says Sam.

He's obviously desperate not to miss a thing, so I agree, even if I am hungry.

We walk through the play park, past Mike's Music Mine and across Highgate. There's a gang of boys from my school outside the sweet shop, and when they see us they start doing monkey impressions. I hope Sam doesn't notice; he gets enough stick at school for having a famous dad with his own personal clone.

Elvis (Dad) + Ziggy = identical twin brothers =
Power of Now (Platinum recording artists and Mojo Award Winners).

But he does. He pokes out his tongue and they all fall about laughing.

"Ignore them," I say. "It's none of their business."

Sam says, "They're just jealous."

And it's easier to agree. Maybe at some level, Sam's right. Maybe they are jealous of a little kid who has the courage to be himself, to be an individual, rather than hang around in a pointless gang, mocking five-year-olds for kicks. Morons.

"Oi! Gorilla boy!" shouts one of the gang, and I realise it's Alex Watson.

Sam turns around ready to retaliate, but I tag his elbow. "Come on, I'll race you," I say, preferring to run

11

away. He doesn't need asking twice because he's a great runner.

We run through Abbot Hall Car Park, down the Waterside and onto the footbridge across the river. The bridge wobbles under our feet. Sam screams and I laugh, and then I grab his hand and we run the rest of the way together.

When we get onto Aynam Road, the bikes and cars are already going past. Sam squeezes my hand. He is, like, so excited it's actually infectious and nothing else matters. I am just happy to be here.

Kendal Torchlight Procession is this annual thing, second Friday night of September; a splash of colour in the 'auld grey town'. It always starts with a bunch of whacky bikes, classic cars and vintage tractors, followed by marching bands and then the floats, all done up to some theme. This year's theme is Kendal through the Ages. People in chainmail and Henry VIII outfits walk along beside the floats selling irrelevant souvenirs and rattling buckets, collecting money for charity. The charity going to benefit from all the effort this year is South Lakeland Carers. I don't even know who or what that is.

"Can I have a flashing wand?" says Sam, when he sees the souvenir sellers.

My heart sinks. If Alex Watson thinks his monkey hat is funny, imagine what he'll make of Sam waving a glittering fairy wand? But I don't want to say no. Instead, I say, "Look at the balloons!" They are helium filled and shaped like sheep. "Aren't they brilliant?"

"I don't like sheep though," he replies, which is news to me. Back in spring when the new born lambs were in the fields, Sam wanted to see them every day.

"So can I?" he asks. "Can I have a wand and do wizard magic?"

"They've got glow sticks as well. I bet they're reeeally magical."

Sam thinks about this. While he is thinking, we see Curtis Watson. Curtis is in Sam's class. He's Alex Watson's little brother and he has about twenty glow sticks wound around his arm.

"No thanks," Sam says. "I'll just have the wand."

He has that look on his face; the steely grey eyes, the sticky out bottom jaw, the flared nostrils. Sam is nothing if not determined and I know he won't back down. I want to please him, I really do. But Sam + glittery wand + Curtis Watson = total annihilation.

"Oh look, Sam! Tractors," I say. I have to distract him.

"Big deal."

"Why is the tractor magic?" I say.

He ignores me.

"Come on; Dad told me this one."

"I don't care," says Sam.

"Because it went down the road and turned into a field!"

"You're not even funny and anyway, I've heard that one before, a million times." No smile, no laugh, nothing. His eyes are glued to the flashing wand seller. "Please, Daisy?" He tugs at my arm. "I'll help you with the shopping tomorrow and I'll do the washing up all week, even when it's not my turn…"

I am losing the will to live. Not because of what he is promising to do because I know it won't happen, but because he wants it so badly and I know how that feels. His eyes plead with me and desperation seems to tie his skinny little body in knots.

My frozen resolve is about to melt when someone taps me on the shoulder; a gentle tap, almost a stroke, and it feels both firm and tender at the same time. I turn around, and there is Dylan.

Sunshine After Rain
Power of Now: Ziggy Meadows

Dylan Bell has this great big smile all over his tanned face; not just his mouth, but his eyes and his cheeks and chin. Like yellow sunshine.

"Oh my god it's you!" I say.

"And you!" he says, beaming.

He is taller than me now, and when he reaches out for a hug I wrap my arms around him and hug back, a proper long one that seems to last forever and end too soon.

"You've grown!" is about all I can think to say. "Like, about six inches!"

He brushes his hand through his cropped blonde hair. "Not quite," he says. "Maybe three? Four at most."

"I can't believe you're here though," I say. And then we both start laughing and for want of anything better to do, hug again.

I've known Dylan, like, all my life; since before I could talk or walk, and until his family moved away, he was always my friend. We used to play in paddling pools together and dress up in our mums' clothes and play at being spies, crazy scientists and rock stars. We've shared birthdays, two funerals, and a wedding when his mum remarried. And when Sam was born and my life fell apart, Dylan and his mum were there for me while Dad and Uncle Ziggy somehow coped with the rest. So we've been through a lot.

15

But standing here with him, now, feels funny. Different. Apart from the height thing his skin smells like honey, his hair is shorter and blonder and his shoulders broader, but it's not about the physical stuff, it's something else. He feels less like Dylan, and well, more like … a boy.

Sam butts into my thoughts. "It's my birthday on Sunday," he says to Dylan.

"Happy Birthday for Sunday, Killer," Dylan replies.

"I'm going to be six," says Sam.

Dylan puts out his hand for a low five. "Put it there," he says.

Sam slaps hard and laughs.

Dylan winces. "It's good to be back," he says, without any hint of irony whilst nursing his sore hand.

"How long are you staying?" I say.

"Forever?" he says.

"Are you joking?" Because he only moved away last year.

"No," he says. "It's all really sudden or I would have told you. Geoff's job folded so Mum asked her old boss at the Day Centre about coming back to Kendal, and he practically bit her hand off. We drove up this morning."

"Where are you living?"

"At Auntie Cath's, till we find a place of our own. She's off travelling again so the house is empty. I'm starting back at King's on Monday. Cool or what?"

"Does that mean I can beat you up?" says Sam.

Actually, Sam has always adored Dylan. They are the brothers they never had.

"I'll tell you what," says Dylan to Sam, "I'll come round tomorrow and we'll fight to the death. Deal?"

"We're not allowed visitors anymore," says Sam.

Dylan looks to me for an explanation.

I shrug. "Don't ask. It's just Dad being antisocial. Maybe you could fight to the death somewhere else?"

Dylan tilts his head to one side and frowns. He wants me to explain, but I shake my head because a) I don't want to talk about Dad or anything grey and boring, and b) it's a white lie. Dad is being antisocial, but he hasn't exactly put a ban on visitors. That was me. And I did it so that people wouldn't laugh at him for being funny; not funny ha ha, but funny peculiar and embarrassing.

I link my arm into Dylan's. The procession proper has started now. There are people in Tudor fancy dress, and floats done up like castles and giant K shoes, and lots of loud music. We watch for a while and then Dylan says, "So, where's Ebony?"

"We don't like Ebony anymore," says Sam. "Because she's going out with Alex Watson and they've been horrible to Daisy."

"What?" says Dylan. He looks a bit shocked.

I explain briefly about how Ebony has dropped me since the house ban and that she is now going out with Alex. Dylan knows how I feel about Alex.

"What about Emily and Sian?"

I shrug. "I don't really see them either."

"So who are you hanging out with?" says Dylan.

"Me," says Sam, which is pretty much the truth.

There are probably about a dozen questions Dylan wants to ask, but he's too nice. He says, "So it's a good thing I'm back then," putting a positive spin on it.

And I say, "Definitely." Because it's not just good, it's amazing. It's like sunshine after rain, like spring flowers after a cold winter, like waking after a bad dream.

"So can I have a flashing wand or what?" says Sam, bringing me back down to planet Earth.

17

Boulevard of Broken Dreams
Green Day: Tré Cool

It was only when we started at King's that being friends with a boy caused a problem. Not for us, for others; twits with nothing better to do than say, "Is that your girlfriend? Is that your boyfriend?" That kind of thing. So Dylan and I spent less time together. When he moved, we stayed in touch; on Facebook and email mostly, until Dad spilled orange juice on the laptop. We tried letters, but no news + no stamp = no letter = no communication.

I regret it now.

Dylan knows me better than anyone, and he knows Sam too. He knows there's no point in trying to talk Sam out of the wand, and yet he also knows what the stakes are.

"How about we all get one?" he says. "Let's start a trend."

It's like, the BEST solution anyone could have come up with and Sam is quite literally dancing twirls on his tip toes, slapping Dylan's hand with every spin round. I dig in my pocket for the twenty pounds and offer it to Sam. He stops twirling, climbs over the barrier and runs off up the road to catch the souvenir seller.

Dylan and I are left alone. Well, alone in a crowd. The words to one of Dad's songs rocks into my head...

How can I feel blue?
When I'm alone with you...

18

… and I think I probably blush.

"So are you still playing guitar?" I say.

"Sure am, and getting quite good too." Dylan grabs his air guitar and mimes some amazing little riff. It reminds me of how he used to be, eight or nine years ago. "And what about you? Got yourself a band yet?"

"Still looking," I lie.

If I was still playing the drums, there's nothing I would love more than to be in a band because it's all I've ever dreamed of doing. Like, when we were kids, Dylan and I used to play this game called Rock 'n Roll Star where we acted out being Dad and Ziggy in Power of Now. Dylan was always Dad because he liked the idea of being a guitarist, and I was always Ziggy because drum kit has been my passion forever. We used to let other kids be the bassist or keyboard player, and we took it in turns to sing. We pretended to be really famous, practised our autographs for fans in home made autograph books, and even planned our UK tour using an AA Map of the Road! It all feels a bit weird now. I mean, Dad's band have split up and we're not kids anymore.

I link my arm into Dylan's and give it a squeeze. "I'm glad you're back," I say. "I've missed you."

He looks into my eyes and is about to speak, but a whistle rips the air. The samba drummers are coming, with jugglers and stilt walkers and women wearing incredible costumes and towering golden head decorations. Suddenly, it feels like a party and we start dancing and clapping to the beat along with everyone else.

Sam races back with three flashing wands and some change. He climbs over the barrier and starts to do silly dancing, looking happier than I've seen him in ages. We wave our wands and in this moment of music and fun, I don't care what anyone thinks.

Cut to the Chase
Rush: Neil Peart

After a while, the traffic stops moving. There is a bottleneck at Miller Bridge and a gap between the floats in front of us.

I look through the gap and there, standing next to Curtis Watson is big brother Alex and the girl who used to be my friend, Ebony Edmonds. They are looking at us and laughing. I lower my fairy wand and cringe inside. Sam and Dylan are still waving theirs about wildly.

"Oi! Gorilla!" calls Alex.

Ebony cackles like a witch and little Curtis shouts something about gays and fairies. His words stab right into my happy heart. I look at Ebony and plead with my eyes. I'm trying to say, give us a break, eh? Sam's just a little kid. But Ebony doesn't get it, or else she pretends not to. I look back at Sam and for all his silly dancing, crazy headgear wearing and fairy wand waving, he's not hurting anyone.

I turn back to Alex and mouth, "Grow. Up."

But Alex takes this as an invitation to be an idiot, and he jumps over the barrier, closely followed by Ebony and Curtis.

"Oh spare me," I say, out loud.

Sam and Dylan turn to see what I see.

"They're coming over here," says Sam, obviously freaked out by this whole new scenario. He grabs my arm. "Let's go. Please, Daisy."

I grab Sam's wrist and we start running; Dylan too. We run towards Miller Bridge and at a break in the barriers, dive behind the Lakeland float and across the road, towards Gooseholme. Sam is out of breath and wants to stop so Dylan grabs hold of his other wrist and tries to make a game of it. He doesn't even really know why we're running.

When we get to the pitch and putt hut, I dare to look back. No sign of the Watsons or Ebony. We take a breather, leaning against the slatted wooden wall. Across the river, the pipe bands of the Royal Scottish Fusiliers are playing All You Need is Love and the procession starts moving again.

Sam says, "Can we go home?"

I say, "Don't you want to watch the rest from Wildman Street?"

"Yeah, come on, Sam," says Dylan. "We'll look after you. There's a load more to see yet."

The way Dylan says 'we', meaning me and him, makes it feel as if we're a couple or something which is, like, a totally weird thought.

Sam peers around the side of the hut looking for the Watsons, but we have definitely lost them.

"Well?" says Dylan.

Sam pulls a thinking face. "I know," he says, as if a light bulb has just lit up some darker recess of his brain. "Instead of watching the Torchlight, we could do that spy game we used to do before you moved, Dylan."

Dylan laughs. He throws his head back and raises one eyebrow and looks at Sam, all suave and sophisticated. "The name's Bond. James Bond."

The pair of them burst into rounds of pretend shooting with their flashing wands, and when they don't stop, I aim my own wand at Dylan and join in.

Dylan grabs his chest and falls into a forward roll before leaping up and diving behind the bench for shelter.

It's a silly game, and we play up and down the river bank, shooting and tagging each other for, like, ten or fifteen minutes. It's probably more fun than the Torchlight and we only stop because Sam is reduced to giggling uncontrollably at Dylan's dramatic falls.

The main thing is, he has stopped worrying about the Watsons, and so have I.

Yellow
Coldplay: Will Champion

With chips and coke, we walk home the long way.

"So are you going to tell me?" says Dylan. "Why were we running away?"

I explain how I beat Watson in the drum-off at Mike's Music Fest in Abbot Hall Park, in front of several hundred people.

"Well that won't make you very popular with Mr Ego," says Dylan.

"Yeah," says Sam. "Daisy was awesome. Best drummer in the whole world."

I'm touched by Sam's faith in me, even though he is talking rubbish.

"Well obviously you beat him," says Dylan. "It's a no brainer."

"No brainer!" says Sam, giggling again. "Alex is a no brainer!"

"He didn't seriously think he'd win though did he?"

"Probably," I say. "Because he made himself look pretty stupid telling everyone before the competition how girls are useless drummers."

"He told everyone Daisy was a cheat," says Sam.

Dylan made a face. "That's not nice."

"He said I only won because of Dad and Ziggy being friends with Mike…"

"They're not though," says Sam. "Dad doesn't even have friends anymore."

"Mike said Watson was just a sore loser and to take no notice…"

"Except he's spread it all round Kendal that Daisy is a cheat…"

"That's ridiculous," says Dylan.

"Anyway, it doesn't matter," I say. "I'm not friends with Ebony any more and she's going out with Watson and it's just best to avoid them whenever possible."

"He's a stupid bully," says Sam.

"Well he always was a meat-head," says Dylan.

Sam thinks that's very funny too. "Meat-head? Ha ha ha."

"But don't let it get you down," says Dylan. "It'll all blow over in a week or two."

He's too nice to understand how bad it's all got between me and Ebony and Alex. He never falls out with people, and even when they upset him, it's like, one shrug and it's over. If Dylan was a drummer he'd be Will Champion playing Yellow; supportive, thoughtful and totally laid back. That's what I love about him most.

We walk up Beast Banks, just chatting and having a laugh with Sam. It's good to spend time with a person my own age, instead of a small boy and a fifty-two-year-old man.

When we get to my house, Dylan says, "Shall I come in and say hello to Elvis? I mean, he knows me doesn't he? He won't mind."

And I know Dad shouldn't mind Dylan, and it feels all wrong telling him to go away but the truth is, I cringe every time Dad opens his mouth in case he makes some awful joke or he's wearing his clothes over his pyjamas or something. "It's late. Maybe another day?"

He looks disappointed and puts his hand out to touch my face. His fingers feel soft. I never knew that before.

But Sam tugs at my arm. "Come on, Daisy, I'm getting wet," he says.

It is raining hard and until this moment I hadn't even noticed.

"Meet me tomorrow?" says Dylan, and kisses me lightly on the cheek before walking off into the night.

Falling off the Edge of the World
Black Sabbath: Vinny Appice

It's two o'clock in the morning and I am listening to Black Sabbath on my iPod, in bed.

I can't sleep because I'm watching the rain on my bedroom windows. I'm remembering Dylan's honeyed smell and wondering why I'd notice that after all this time. I'm looking at the drum kit in the corner of my room; untouched in months, and covered in dust. I'm thinking about how Carla Azar the Autolux drummer, fell off a stage, shattered her elbow and was told she'd never drum again. Several hours of surgery and a handful of titanium screws later, she was back at the kit as if she'd never been away. And I'm playing with the idea of getting back on my own kit, just like I've never been away. Anything is possible.

Between tracks, I hear a noise outside in the front garden. I'd like to ignore it because I wouldn't put it past Watson and his meat-head mates to pull up our plants or something; just for a laugh. But I can't.

I get up, move back the curtains, and see Dad. He is wearing his blue pyjamas and holey slippers, and he is leaning over the wheelie bin. He's had trouble sleeping since Mum died and I guess he's putting the rubbish out. It's the kind of thing he does these days. But he falls, backwards. I don't know how or why. I grab my dressing gown and run downstairs and out into the front garden.

He's sitting there on the wet grass, in the rain, looking at his hands.

"Are you all right?" I say.

"I can't find it," he says.

"Can't find what?" I say.

"That damned wallet. I know I had it."

I feel guilty then. "It's okay," I say. "We found it in the fridge."

"The fridge? What silly sod puts a wallet in the fridge?"

"Beats me," I say, supporting his elbow while he stands. I take him inside and fetch a clean towel from the airing cupboard. "Are you all right? Did you hurt yourself?" I say, wrapping the towel around his shoulders.

"I'm not a baby," he says. "I can do things for myself." He yanks the towel from me and starts to dry his hair.

"Sorry," I say, "I was trying to help."

"Then you should have told me about the wallet. I haven't slept a wink all night," he says. "Where is it now?"

"Your coat pocket," I say.

"Okay. Well no more hiding it in the fridge. You understand?" he says. "You know what I'm like."

I bite my tongue, apologise again and go back to bed.

It's two-thirty in the morning. I am listening to Black Sabbath on my iPod, and watching the raindrops on my bedroom windows, wondering why they look so much like tears.

Numb
Linkin Park: Rob Bourdon

We always do shopping on a Saturday. Ever since Sam was a baby we've done it. It used to be a treat. Dad would say, "Help me choose some delicious delights," and we'd wander around the supermarket putting everything we fancied in the basket. Week after week we ended up with crisps, cakes, chocolate and jelly.

But after a while, Ziggy said we should think about a more sensible diet (because he was very into his vegetables, tofu and beans). Dad and Ziggy fell out over that and we didn't see Ziggy for a few days. When he came back, Dad said it wouldn't hurt if we knew how to do things properly and let Ziggy show us how to make menus and write lists and stuff. We used to sit down together, the three of us, me and Dad and Ziggy, and plan for the week. I pretty much do it on my own now. It's not because I'm the girl; it's just because Dad is so hopeless and Ziggy isn't here.

This week, it's different. All three of us are going; a family outing. Whoopee! Sam promised to help last night, plus, it's his birthday tomorrow so he'll want to choose a birthday cake. Dad has also decided to help.

Sam pushes the trolley, which is always risky, but easier than letting him find the food. I give Dad half the list and take the other half for myself. Sam is supposed to wait in the middle of the two sets of aisles so that we can put the stuff in the basket.

But Dad's confused because they've changed the layout and he doesn't know where to find things. So I tell him to mind the trolley instead, and send Sam off to choose a birthday cake. I zoom around with the full list.

I am about to choose bubble bath for Sam, when he skips back to me, holding a caterpillar cake and a Spiderman cake, singing, "We're getting a puppy, we're getting a puppy."

"Er, no. We're not," I say.

"Then why is Dad buying dog food?" he says.

"He's what?"

I march to the pet food aisle, and see Dad reading the labels on tins of dog meat.

"Can we get one though?" says Sam, skipping along beside me.

"No," I say, whilst trying to work out what Dad is thinking.

"Because Dan's got a dog," says Sam. Dan is in Sam's class. "It's black and it poos in the house and…"

"Stop!" I say. I can't be having a conversation about dogs or puppies or poo. There is no way we are getting a pet.

When we reach Dad, I say, "What are you doing?"

"Just looking. Because I used to have a dog; when I was a kid," Dad says.

"I know."

"He looked just like this." There's a picture of a small white and brown dog on the Chappie tin, smiling. "Shifty, we called him. That wasn't his real name. His real name was Prince, but you couldn't trust him around food or he'd nick it; soon as you turned your back he was in there; off your plate, off the table, out of the fridge. Didn't care what he ate as long as he stole it. Hence, Shifty."

30

It feels rude to tell Dad I've heard this story a hundred times, but I tell him anyway because the shopping won't do itself and I would really like to get home and phone Dylan.

"I'm being boring am I?" he says, a twinkle in his eye, putting the Chappie tin back on the shelf.

"No," I say. "You're not boring," which is true. He may be embarrassing, but he's never boring. How many other kids can say their Dad writes songs for a living, has been on TV, toured the world in a rock group and met Lars Ulrich, Bill Ward and Nicko McBrain? "It's just that I'd like to get finished because I'm meeting a friend."

Dad raises his eyebrows in, like, a question mark. He expects me to elaborate.

"Dylan," I say. "He's moved back to Kendal. Isn't that brilliant?"

"Dylan who?"

"Dylan Bell."

Dad looks blankly at me.

"Dylan and Elaine? You can't have forgotten them. They moved to London after Elaine married Geoff."

"Oh yes, I knew that," says Dad.

I wish he would listen properly.

At the checkout, Sam prefers to play in the photo booth, leaving us to pack. Me and Dad work super quickly, with Dad unloading onto the conveyor belt and me filling the bags at the other end. When everything is through, Dad gives me his wallet and I pay with his credit card. We do it like this because Dad is scatty about numbers, and he's been known to forget his PIN, which is mega embarrassing and means we have to leave with no shopping.

The checkout lady gives me a funny look. I'm thinking she must know it's not my card and I shouldn't be using it, but wondering what she can do. I mean, it's not as if Dad isn't here is it? But I see her eyes sort of flick from me to Dad and instinctively, follow them.

Dad is unpacking the shopping I have already packed.

"What are you doing?" I say.

Walking past our checkout I see Ebony and her sister, Misha.

Dad stops unpacking and looks at me, then the shopping and back at me. Dad is like, in a world of his own.

"I've just packed that," I say, trying to ignore Ebony.

And then Dad realises what he's doing. "Sorry," he says. "Miles away."

Ebony and Misha have a good laugh at our expense. It's times like these when I wish I could leave Dad at home.

Waiting
Green Day: Tré Cool

I am meeting Dylan in Maccy D's. I am first to arrive and sit in a seat near the window where I can see up the road. The smell of the food makes me hungry, but I resist the temptation because I'd rather wait for Dylan.

He's late.

People are staring at me. Rudy, a boy who used to go to my school, is wiping tables and clearing away. Apparently I'm not supposed to sit without a purchase, but Rudy is nice about it; says it's only the manager who cares. So I go the counter and buy a cup of tea, leaving my coat to save the seat.

"Still drumming?" says Rudy. He knows I am a drummer because he is too.

"Yeah," I lie. We played against each other in the drum-off and he was pretty good – very metal, and really physical. Technically you couldn't fault him, but he needs to play down, to let up, feel the dynamics a bit more.

"I'm at the college now," he says. "Doing the music BTEC. You get put in different bands, play different styles and we do a load of gigs. It's awesome. You'd love it."

"Sounds like fun," I say.

"Serious fun. Do you play anything else?"

I tell him I used to play keyboard and a bit of guitar, and that when Mum was alive I used to like singing.

"Then you should do the BTEC too. They'd love you. All that talent *and* a rock pedigree," he winks. There's something really x-factor about him. I mean, he's not my type, but he is good looking and friendly and maybe a bit like Dylan. And he does kind of make me think I shouldn't put off my dream.

I walk away, smiling and dreaming about being the next Cindy Blackman, in a world of my own. Until I see Ebony. She is at my table with a bunch of girls I don't recognise. My coat is on the floor.

"Oh sorry," says Ebony, all innocent and butter-wouldn't-melt, like. "Is that yours? I thought it was a cleaning rag!" Her friends laugh.

I don't even bother to answer. I just pick up my coat and go outside. She calls my name, but I ignore her.

A Kind of Magic
Queen: Roger Taylor

I wait on a wooden bench with my cup of tea, and try not to think about Ebony. She is so not worth it.

Instead, I wonder about doing the music BTEC. How cool would it be to play in loads of bands and start gigging? I'm smiling, imagining me at the back, keeping time, totally rapt in the music, but waiting for my solo… and then it comes…1 and, 2 and, 1 2 3 4 … sticks hit skins and I'm giving it out like Travis Barker on a good day…

In the middle of this daydream, Dylan arrives.

"Sorry sorry sorry," he says. "Mum wanted me to look at a house with her. I didn't think … Hang on, what are you smiling at?" He flattens his hair, in case I'm laughing at him or something.

I say, "Nothing important," and change the subject. "Tell me about this house."

"It was up near yours," he says. "Vale Crescent?"

"Are you going to move in?" It is literally round the corner from me. Just the thought of that makes me feel stupidly happy.

"I wish," he says. "But apparently we don't need four bedrooms." He does this pretend pout thing which makes me laugh, and then asks if we're going to get food.

I explain about Ebony being in Maccy D's and Dylan gets it straight away.

"So let's just go for a walk," he says.

I'm not even hungry anymore, so I drop my tea-cup in a bin and we walk off towards the river. We walk down Sandes Avenue and onto the footpath beside the water. It's nice, just the two of us. The leaves are beginning to turn on the trees and the air is fresh. I like autumn. I like river walks and obviously, I like Dylan.

We talk mostly about all the school gossip he's missed; who's going out with who, which teachers have left and how Stacey Wilson in our year got sent to live with a foster family when her Mum got really ill. We both think about how terrible this would be, and how lucky we are that our families managed to pull together and cope when things were bad for us.

Then Dylan tells me all about his time down South and the people he met and his school and having Chinese food in the real Chinatown in London and how it's warmer and friendlier and ... well loads of stuff. I get a real sense that he misses it and he'd rather be there. I don't blame him. Kendal must be so dull after London.

We cross the suspension bridge and I catch sight of ripples, and something moving in the water below. "Oh my god did you see that? Was it an otter?" I know there are otters here but I've never, in all my life, like, seen one for real. I point to where it was and Dylan looks but it's too late. "It was an otter, I'm sure it was an otter," I say.

We stand on the bridge for ages, completely silent so as not to scare anything, hoping we'll see it again. We see a couple of salmon jumping, and birds, and plenty of dog walkers. Someone jogs past with a dog the same breed as Shifty, but we don't see the otter again, and give up. We cross over onto the other side and walk along the path to Sandy Bottoms.

It's muddy, and we don't say much because we're concentrating on not slipping over. But suddenly I see it again; the otter. "Look!" I shout and point to the opposite bank of the river where there are lots of boulder stones. The otter is there, holding something in his paws, eating. A fish.

"Oh wow!" cries Dylan.

The otter is startled by our squeals and slides back into the river. We watch it disappear up stream. But it's like, magical. Totally magical. Amazing. An injection of bliss. To see something so rare and so special, with Dylan. I am on a high. The only word that comes out of my mouth is "WOW!" Just WOW.

And Dylan is obviously feeling the same because we both walk around Sandy Bottoms punctuating our dirty great smiles with, "Wow!" We see cormorants, a heron and plenty of rabbits, but nothing is as special as the otter. When we've done the loop and get back to the suspension bridge we stand a while, hoping to see it again, but that would be too much luck for one day. It doesn't matter.

When we reach town, Dylan says, "It's good to be back. London wasn't nearly as exciting as Kendal."

Birthday
The Beatles: Ringo Starr

Sam's birthday present is a trip to Dalton Zoo. Me and Dad chose it together after Sam saw some kangaroos on TV and fell in love. When Dad told us he'd seen real live kangaroos on a beach in Australia during the Power of Now tour, Sam was, like, "Can we go to Australia? Please can we go to Australia? I love kangaroos. I'm going to marry a kangaroo..." and hopping about the place as if he was one.

Me and Dad thought it would be cool if he actually saw one for real, and Dalton Zoo is the next best thing to Australia. So first of all, we adopted one for ten pounds a year. Then we got him a cuddly toy kangaroo and put it in a shoe box with the adoption certificate, and then we wrapped it all up in blue tissue paper and stuck loads of curled up silver curling ribbon on top. (Well, I did the ribbon.) Dad chose a card with a picture of a monkey on the front, and inside the card he wrote...

To Sam,
This is not a birthday card.
It's a Zoo token!!!
Valid at Dalton Zoo, for 3 people.

We both signed it and I put lots of kisses, and Dad bought a little badge with I am 6 written on it.

Sam was very excited in bed last night and I am sure he will be awake early, so I set my alarm to be up even earlier. I don't want him nosing around and opening his surprise before we give it to him.

Downstairs, Dad is already awake and dressed, and the table is laid for breakfast. He's wearing a silly old Napoleon hat from the dressing up box and has decorated the kitchen with balloons. Dad's probably the biggest kid in our family.

I can see the oven is on. "What are you cooking?" I say.

"Oven chips," he says.

"Awesome! Chips for breakfast. That's a proper treat."

Dad stops and looks through me for a while, and then at his watch. He says, "Yeah, a treat."

Sometimes we have these conversations that don't make a lot of sense, but it doesn't matter. I get Sam's present and put it on the table and when the chips are ready, we give him a call.

He bounces out of his room and down the stairs like an over excited puppy; he's obviously been waiting for this moment. When he sees the balloons, the wrapped up present and the plate of chips, he is like, "Wow!" and "Oh Man!" and "Crazy!" He rushes up to Dad and gives him such a big hug he almost falls backwards, and then he high fives me – a little more gently than usual – before starting on his food.

Between mouthfuls, he opens his present. The kangaroo is perfect. He calls it Martin; I don't know why. And then he sees the adoption certificate and opens the card and he cannot believe we are having a day out. "Us three?" he says.

"That's right."

"Are you coming?" he says to Dad.

"Yes!" I say. "Sam plus Daisy plus Dad makes us three."

And Sam's all, "Wow!" and "Oh Man!" and "Crazy!" again. I can't really remember the last time we had a *proper* family outing; certainly not since Dad lost his driving licence, and I'm really looking forward to it as well. (As long as we don't see anyone we know.)

The Main Monkey Business
Rush: Neil Peart

Because it's a Sunday, the bus journey takes forever. I listen to music, but Dad and Sam play I-Spy out of the window. Sam gives really easy I-Spies, such as "I spy with my mince pie something beginning with S."

"Sky," says Dad, straight off. And of course he's right.

Dad lets Sam have lots of goes because they are all like that, (R – for road, Sh – for sheep, Gr – for grass...) but also because it's Sam's birthday.

When his clues start to get silly, (W – for worm, B – for Bum, Th – for thinking) I suggest that Dad has a turn.

"I spy with my little eye, something beginning with S," says Dad.

Sam says, "Spider, seats, sausages, sun, sky..."

"That's it," says Dad. "Sky."

"But I did that one," says Sam.

"Did you?" says Dad.

"That was my first one."

"Does it matter?" says Dad.

"Do another one," I suggest.

So Dad looks around and says, "I spy with my little eye, something beginning with W."

Sam says, "Window, walls, worm..." and can't think of anything else. He looks all around for inspiration. Dad opens a packet of sweets and offers me one. We go through Ulverston, with Sam saying, "Um... um..." and I try and think of some answers to help him.

"Woman? Writing?" I say, but Dad just sits there laughing.

In the end, Sam says, "Give us a clue."

And Dad's face creases into a kind of awkward frown. "I've forgotten!" he says.

"What?"

"You took too long!" he says.

Sam just thinks this is hilarious and starts to pretend punch Dad, but he's laughing at the same time so I can see he doesn't really mind.

When we get to Dalton Zoo, there is a little train you can sit on and go for a ride. It's not very far, and Sam is dead keen, but I don't really want a go. It's more for kids than people my age. Dad says he'll go with Sam, so I hang around in the shop, buy a map of the zoo and some drinks for when they have finished, then wait at the end of the track for them to return.

As the train gets close, I hear Dad and Sam singing, "We're going to the zoo, zoo, zoo. How about you, you, you..." and other people, like, total strangers, are joining in. "You can come too, too, too. We're going to the zoo!"

I look around to make sure there is nobody I know, but secretly, I am well proud of Dad for making it such a happy day for Sam.

We sit and have our drinks and look at the map. Sam wants to see everything; lions, giraffes, hippos, rhinos, tigers, monkeys, lemurs, the birds... everything. But first, we have to visit the kangaroos.

There are a couple of big red kangaroos and some smaller grey ones, and there are a lot of wallabies too, but they are all just standing around eating, or lying down.

"Why aren't they hopping about?" says Sam.

"Because they're eating," I say.

We stand and watch them some more, but even when they do move, it's just the odd step or two and not very dramatic. This isn't what Sam was expecting and I can see the disappointment on his face.

So can Dad. "What do you get if you cross an elephant with a kangaroo, Sam?" he says, trying to lighten the mood.

"I don't know."

"Great big holes all over Australia!" says Dad.

Sam half laughs, but he's not very impressed. It's not the same as a jumping kangaroo. He stares at the Big Red and I know he's willing it to start hopping about.

"Okay, what about this one?" says Dad. "Why did the kangaroo cross the road?"

"I don't know," says Sam.

And I'm, like, please let this be funny, because Dad is trying really hard here.

Dad says, "Because it was the chicken's day …"

But Sam shouts, "Look!"

We both look at the kangaroo and something sticks out of her pouch. It's a tiny bony leg. The mum kangaroo looks down and kind of pokes it back in the pouch, but the leg pops out again almost immediately. It's hilarious.

"Look! Look!" says Sam. He is practically glued to the spot, staring at this small miracle. "She's having a baby!" he says.

A little grey head pops out then, followed by another leg, and finally the rest of its body flops out onto the ground. It's skinny and really funny, and hops a couple of wobbly hops, then turns around and climbs back into the pouch.

"Oh man! Did you see that? Did you see that? Oh wow! That was amazing!" Sam turns to Dad and gives him the biggest hug, as if Dad was personally responsible for laying on this spectacle. And I suppose, in a way he was.

We stand and watch for the joey to pop out again, but it doesn't. The zoo keeper tells us she is a female joey and she's about six months old, having spent four months in the pouch suckling. He says it's still pretty rare to see her and that we've been very lucky. We couldn't have wished for better timing.

Dad buys us lunch in the café. Sam has chips for the second time today. He also has ice cream and chocolate and a bag of sweets.

And afterwards we race around trying to see all the other animals before closing time. Sam loves everything, but his absolute favourite (after the joey kangaroo) is the spider monkey whose tail works like another arm, picking things up and holding onto branches when it swings in the trees.

It's been the nicest day we have had in a long time, and it doesn't matter that we miss the bus home and have to get a taxi. It doesn't matter that we have to ask the driver to stop because Sam is feeling sick and needs to throw up. And it doesn't matter that when we get home, Dad puts seven candles on Sam's cake instead of six. It's just been the best day.

Meant to Live
Switchfoot: Chad Butler

My fingers have been crossed all weekend, hoping that Dylan will be in my form. I open the classroom door, but he is not here.

Mrs Pike, our form teacher, looks at me and does one of those *you're late again* sighs, and nods to the nearest chair for me to sit down. Before I have even parked my bum in the seat, a paper aeroplane hits me in the back of the head.

I turn to see Watson smiling like a faker. "Read it then," he says.

I screw the aeroplane into a ball and throw it back, unread. It's just going to say something about fairy wands or *has-been* rock stars anyway. Watson bats it to the floor.

Mrs Pike looks at me. "Pick it up," she says, weary.

I do as I'm asked and throw the ball of paper plane in the bin. Watson relaxes with his arms behind his head and grins.

I sit through double English and IT listening to Watson whispering loud enough for me to hear, "Your brother is gay... Your dad is mental... Girl drummers suck." The teachers don't hear him and no one sticks up for me. No one steps in and says, 'leave her alone' or 'grow up' or any of the things I would do if I saw him bullying someone, and I try to console myself with the thought that it's more about them being scared of him, than anyone hating me. And at least I have a genuine friend now Dylan is back.

When at last the dinner bell rings, I am free! I head for my usual spot on the seat behind the history block. There should be a plaque on it;

Dylan Bell + Daisy Meadows → totally OWN this seat.

We hid here in year seven when the school was a big scary place, and you can almost see the dents where our bums used to be! I sit down, knowing Dylan will find me.

"You all right?" he says, seconds later.

"Better for seeing you," I say.

He sits next to me. I am about to tell him all about our day at the zoo, but half way through telling him, I realise our legs are touching. Our legs must have touched plenty of times when we were kids; it never gave me a racing heart or made me forget my words before. Dylan talks to me, and I'm not really hearing his words because I'm thinking... My Leg + Dylan's Leg. My Leg + Dylan's Leg. My Leg + Dylan's Leg.

I am only brought back to the conversation when Dylan says, "But I'm looking forward to music last lesson. You're doing that too, right?"

Ouch! I would have chosen music if I'd known Dylan was coming back. "I'm not doing music," I say. "I opted for further maths instead."

Dylan laughs. "You're joking."

I almost don't believe it myself. "I'm not joking," I say.

"But how can you, of all people, NOT do music?"

I don't want to tell him I stopped playing the drums because Dad can't stand the noise, in case he joins in with everyone else and thinks Dad is weird. And I don't want to tell him that I refused to do music as a kind of protest thingy, because even I can see it was a pointless over-reaction. The phrase 'cutting off my nose to spite my face' springs to mind, and I could kick myself now. "You know I like maths," I say, hoping he doesn't pick up the terminal regret in my voice.

Dylan does his pout. "But I was so looking forward to doing music with you," he says. "We could have had fun together."

I smile and open my lunch. I'm not hungry for sandwiches and pull out the crisps, thinking what a good thing it is I don't have cheese and onion because I don't want smelly breath. "Do you want one?" I say, trying to change the subject.

"Nah," he says. "I'm just really sad you're not doing it."

I shove too many crisps in my mouth so I don't have to answer. They all break up and crisp crumbs fall onto my sweatshirt. Dylan just laughs and brushes the crisps away for me.

Who Are You?
Who: Keith Moon

Mrs Pike wants to know why I'm not concentrating in maths. I can't tell her, because all I am thinking about is Dylan and music and wondering if it's too late to swap options.

When school ends, I rush to catch Dylan. We literally bump into each other half way between maths and music.

"I was just coming to find you," he says, smiling the kind of smile which makes me feel warm and happy inside.

"And me you," I say.

We link arms, just real natural like, and walk out of school together. He asks about Sam's birthday and we talk about the time we went to Dalton Zoo together when my mum was alive. I barely notice the meat-heads smoking on the wall and with Dylan beside me it's easy to ignore their comments. We walk down to Gooseholme and Dylan points towards a bench, where we sit down. I notice how blue the sky is and how the leaves are beginning to turn orange and red and brown. I don't remember them ever looking this lovely before.

"Have you seen this?" he says, and produces a crumpled A5 flyer from his pocket.

It's an advert for a Battle of the Bands competition in school. I've seen it about a million times already, and every single time it hurts. There's no way I can do it. Mr Strummer announced it last term to give us the summer to practice and polish up our acts. He said he wants real talent to enter, kids who've worked hard to produce something worth performing.

"Let's go for it. We'd be great, you and me. This could be our big chance. We'll get a band together. It's a mega plan!" Dylan's eyes are, like, shining and he's so happy. "Well?" He's waiting for an answer, but I don't have one.

If I tell Dylan the truth, I know he'll argue and make it sound as if there's no problem.

Me: I'm not allowed to play drums anymore.
Dylan: Of course you are. How can anyone stop you?
Me: Because the noise upsets Dad, and I feel a bit stupid telling you that.
Dylan: So? Play somewhere else. It's not like you've lost the use of your arms.

"What are you smiling about now?" says Dylan.

"I was thinking about Rick Allen," I say.

"Who's Rick Allen?"

"Def Leppard drummer. Lost an arm in a car crash and he still plays."

"So how is that relevant?"

I have to laugh. "It just means that if you want something badly enough, you can make it happen," I say.

It's not a Yes and it's not a No. We won't find anyone else who wants to play in a band with me anyway, so it's never going to happen. Dylan victory-punches the air. I haven't exactly deceived him, but I haven't exactly been honest either and I feel bad.

"Do you want to feed the ducks?" I say, to change the subject. I dig in my bag for the sandwiches I didn't eat at lunchtime. "There was a cormorant here last week, drying out his wings on the rocks. Cormorants do eat cheese sandwiches, don't they?"

"Of course they do," says Dylan. "It's just about their favourite meal." He tears off a crust of bread and throws it high into the air.

A flock of seagulls and pigeons immediately surround us. Dylan holds my arm out and balances a piece of bread on the back of my hand. Almost immediately, a pigeon lands there and starts to peck at the bread. I stand as still as can be and watch. It's so cute.

"Stay like that," he says, reaching into his own bag.

"I'll take your picture on my phone. Or shall I take it on your phone?"

"Don't have one..." I say. And I'm about to tell him how I lost it when the shrill voice of Ebony Edmonds stops me.

"Yeughhhh..." she cries. "A skanky pigeon."

The pigeon flies away.

"Thanks," I say, sarcastically.

"Pleasure," says Ebony.

Dylan ignores her, but she's spoiled a moment in my life when everything was just perfect.

And I know I should just forget it, but I don't want to. I am actually really fed up with Ebony and Watson.

"Why don't you just get lost?" I say.

And Ebony bursts out laughing. "What, like Elvis?"

Before Dad got banned from driving and Ebony was at my house, Dad phoned up to say he was lost. He'd been to Carlisle to meet an old friend and missed the motorway turning back into Kendal, because it was dark and he got confused about where he was. I had to

50

google directions for him from Preston back home. Ebony has never let me forget it.

"You're so not funny," I say.

"But your dad is. LOL!" she says. Then she turns to Watson and tells him how she'd seen us at the supermarket. "So there was Daisy packing all the shopping into the bags and there was Elvis taking it all out again. Totally comical."

It's not, comical. But I don't know how to stop them laughing. Dad did do that and I can't say otherwise, but it's not funny. It's annoying and embarrassing and even a bit weird, but it's not funny and I don't have a comeback. Tears prickle my eyes and I turn away.

Dylan sees my upset and stands between me and Ebony. "Don't be so horrible," he says, to Ebony. He's calm and reasonable, and asks, "What's the point in being mean?"

Ebony doesn't have an answer. She just stands there, with her mouth open, trying to pretend she's not shocked that someone is at last on my side.

"Leave 'er alone," butts in Watson. "You got something to say, say it to me."

And then Dylan reacts. It takes me by surprise. "Yes I have got something to say. I know about the drum-off and I heard you were a bad loser. But anyone with an ounce of brain can see Daisy is way better than you," says Dylan, adding "Loser," under his breath.

But not under enough for Watson to miss. "Who are you calling Loser?"

Dylan doesn't answer with words; he points. And the point becomes a poke, and Watson steps back. He's surprised. We're all surprised. But Dylan keeps poking and Watson keeps backing off till he reaches the wet grass, loses his footing and falls to the ground.

51

Dylan turns away and starts to walk back to me but before he's done even a couple of steps, Watson is on his feet and lunging at Dylan.

I scream, and manage to whack Watson around the head with my school bag. Watson falls flat on the tarmac. It's almost funny. But only for a moment, because Watson jumps up again and lurches towards me. Ebony is screaming and I'm preparing myself for Watson to hit me, when Dylan gets between us again and lands a killer punch, right in Watson's stomach. Watson doubles up on the grass, gasping for breath.

I swear I've never seen anything like it in my whole life. I feel sick. I didn't want this to happen and I don't know where it came from.

Ebony picks Watson up and he's, like, wheezing and swearing and trying not to cry, and they start to walk away. I look at Dylan. He has blood coming from his nose. I wipe it with my hanky, trying not to hurt.

"Oh. My. God," I say. "I can't believe you just did that."

And Dylan laughs; a nervous and shaky laugh. "Neither can I!"

Nobody's Fault but Mine
Led Zeppelin: John Bonham

I get into registration late. Everyone is leaving as I arrive.

"Ah, Daisy. Nice of you to put in an appearance," says Mrs Pike. Teachers must do a special course in sarcasm.

I apologise and get jeers and sneers off certain people who are also frequently late, only not as late as me today.

"Do you have a reason?" says Mrs Pike. "For your lateness."

I shrug and mumble something about the alarm not going off.

Watson cheers. Like, he's never used that excuse? I'm hardly going to tell the whole class that Dad's nocturnal wanderings kept me from sleeping again.

"There's a note for you," she says, opening the register and taking out a piece of paper. "Here."

The note is from Miss Canning, the Headmaster's secretary, inviting me to the Head's office at the end of registration. I'm guessing that Mrs Pike is finally going to do something about my lateness.

The Head is Mr Badger. Most pupils go through their whole school life without ever seeing the inside of his office and until now, I thought I was one of them.

"Hello Daisy," says Miss Canning, his secretary. She is smiling and upbeat, and it puts me at ease a little. "Mr Badger is busy. Please wait over there." She nods at the grey plastic chairs and I sit down. Miss Canning leaves with a pile of papers and I am alone.

There are posters and pictures on the walls, advertising school activities and events, and there is one for the Battle of the Bands competition. Just for a minute I allow myself to dream about being up there, on stage; Daisy Meadows, the World's Greatest Drummer. I grab a couple of pencils from Miss Canning's pencil pot and start practising triple paradiddles on the back of a chair. Right Left Right Left Right Left Right Right, Left Right Left Right Left Right Left Left … keeping 4:4 time and concentrating on the phrasing. It's still easy. I've still got it.

But Mr Badger's door opens and interrupts my fantasy life.

A tall dark haired woman comes out, dressed smart, in a proper coat and high heels, followed by a girl my age, with crazy black hair, thick mascara and a pierced nose. Behind them, Mr Badger looks short and round by comparison. Mr Badger glares at me and I hide the pencils under my leg.

"Any concerns, Mrs Scarponi," he says, to the woman. "Ring me. I'm always happy to speak to parents."

The woman turns to the girl and holds out her hand. "Loretta, your nose?" she says.

I have to stifle a laugh. Loretta looks at me and rolls her eyes, as if her mum is a real drag, and then slowly removes the nose stud; a little black pin with a cone shaped end.

The mum says, "This is a new start for us, Loretta. Let's make it work," and then leans forward and brushes cheeks, first one then the other. "Ciao," she says.

Loretta raises her eyebrows. The mum and Mr Badger say goodbye, shaking hands, reassuring each other of Loretta's potential and the school's commitment to excellence. The mum leaves. Mr Badger tells me to wait, then disappears with the new girl. I take out my pencils and try my triples for speed, starting slow and getting faster. It's like, the most fun you can have with pencils.

But Ebony appears around the corner and comes to sit next to me. I stop. She sneers. Neither of us speaks, and it is actually a relief when Badger returns.

Inside his office, he says, "Do you know why you're here?"

"Because I've been late a few times?" I say.

Mr Badger says, "Well I am concerned about your punctuality, it's true." He stares at me, takes a breath and says, "But something else entirely is the main reason you're here."

I know I haven't been, like, totally meticulous about getting my homework done and my uniform's not always exactly perfect, but I don't think they are serious enough to warrant Badger getting on my case.

"You were involved in a fight, on Gooseholme. Correct?"

So that's why Ebony is outside. I want to protest and say I didn't start it, but it's not a good idea to argue, so I just nod.

"Well I'm disappointed, Daisy," he says. "I used to think of you as one of our most promising students. Your marks were consistently high; you were enthusiastic about school and produced some excellent work. But more and more over the last year, I have been listening to comments from your teachers about you failing to hand in homework, not paying attention in class and this constant issue of lateness. Would you say that's fair?"

It is, I suppose; I just haven't really thought about it like that. I shrug and mumble my agreement.

"And now this issue of fighting. It's not like you, Daisy, and it troubles me." He pauses, shuffles some papers on his desk and then says, "Would you like to tell me what's going on?"

"Nothing's going on," I say.

"You see, Daisy. A year or two ago, I would never have believed it if someone had told me they'd seen you fighting. But I'm afraid, now I'm not surprised. In my experience, students don't usually change their personalities unless there is a specific issue which needs dealing with." He looks at my face. I think he's gauging my reaction. "Perhaps bullying? Or sometimes the culprit is a problem at home."

I don't know how to react. "Nothing's wrong," I say. "I just... I just..." But I can't think of an excuse because there isn't one. That'd be like Lenny Kravitz playing out of tune and Cindy Blackman saying it made her a bad drummer. Just because life sucks sometimes, it doesn't mean I have to. "I'm sorry," I say. "I'll try harder."

Mr Badger doesn't say anything. The room is silent and uncomfortable and I don't know where to look. He's got cups and medals in a large glass cabinet. There are pictures of kids who've been in the Gazette and certificates on the wall. And on his desk there's a lump of coloured glass, papers and pens lined up in order of size, all neat and tidy. He likes things neat and tidy does Mr Badger. He likes his rules and his league tables and his 91% of students with A - C passes at GCSE.

"Right," he says, making me jump. "Leave this with me. I'd like to speak to your father. I'll call him this afternoon and we'll take it from there. You may go back to class."

Shiny Happy People
REM: Bill Berry

I sit on the seat by the history block in drizzling rain. It's that thin watery mist you can't get away from, so there's no point sheltering under the awnings. I am longing to see Dylan, to tell him what's happened and ask if he's in trouble too.

I open my lunch, starting with the cheese and lettuce sandwich. The bread's dry because even though we went shopping on Saturday, we somehow managed to buy two cakes and no bread. Sam wanted bubble bath and we forgot that too.

Loretta comes over and sits next to me. I am tempted to save the space for Dylan and be on my own, but I don't get a chance.

"Cool drumming," says Loretta. "It was driving that Head bloke insane."

"Thanks," I say.

"He kept looking at the door. Had to stop myself from laughing out loud. You should take it up," she says.

"Take what up?"

"Drums. You're a natch."

It makes me laugh. Everyone in Kendal knows I play the drums. (Correction: used to play the drums.) Small town. And because of Dad and Ziggy, everyone knows me; if not to talk to, then at least to point at. It's like, refreshing to be unknown, and a part of me wants it to stay that way.

"I play bass," she says. "Used to be in a band; the Metallic Babes. Metal, obs. We was rubbish." Loretta throws back her head and laughs. "Never did no gigs or nothing. Practised in my mate's bedroom. Alice. She was the drummer. Blew all the lectrics in her house and couldn't hear nothing 'cept drums. Hilare! And another time Shannon fell over the amp, moshing; broke her arm and that. We was in stitches. Till we realised, and then we was all oh em gee she's really hurt and everything…"

Loretta obviously doesn't expect me to speak, so I relax a little and just enjoy her stories about the Metallic Babes and their disasters. I think I like her. She's kind of on the edge; different from the other girls round here and it's very entertaining.

"… I miss 'em though. Still in touch and everything, but I need a new band; something to get my teeth into …"

Just as I am about to take a bite from my sandwich, I spot some bluey green mould spots on the crust. "Gross!" I say, ripping them off.

Loretta doesn't comment. She tells me about her old school in Colchester and where she's living now and how she wants to be a rock star and how her gran knew Suzi Quatro (who is, like, this seventies bass playing rock chick) and how she can't wait till her mum agrees that she's old enough to go to festivals.

But suddenly I see Dylan across the yard and I stop listening. He is talking to Matt, one of his friends before the move. When he sees me he waves. I wave back, and he comes over to us.

He smiles at me and introduces himself to Loretta. "You're the new girl," he says. "I'm Dylan. Hi!"

"Loretta," she says. "Hi!"

I expect her to go rambling on about Colchester and girl-bands and her gran's best friend again, but she doesn't say a word.

Dylan squeezes between us on the bench and turns to me. "I got a right telling off for fighting in school uniform!" he says. "What about you?"

"Mr Badger wants to talk to my dad," I say.

Dylan's face scrunches up. "What for?"

I shrug. "He thinks I've had a personality transplant or something."

"Oh em gee!" says Loretta. "That is so hilaire. It's exactly what my mum said to me when I joined the Babes." She laughs her laugh again and Dylan gives me a sideways look. He's confused.

"Loretta was in a band called the Metallic Babes at her last school," I explain. "She plays bass."

"Guitar," says Loretta. "Not upright. I ain't nearly jazzy enough for that. LOL! No, I'm metal, obs."

"You play bass?" says Dylan, taking an interest in Loretta all of a sudden. I know what he's thinking. He's thinking *potential band member*. "I play guitar. Daisy plays drums."

"So you *are* a drummer?" she says to me. "I knew it. I could tell. That's ace. What do you like? Metal? Thrash? Punk? And there was me thinking this place would be a total backwater, but oh em gee this is amazo! A drummer and a guitarist, on my first day! The Babes will be well jel." Loretta puts her hand on Dylan's thigh. She has long fingers and shiny red nail polish.

Dylan looks at the hand and shifts uncomfortably. "Anyway," says Dylan, suddenly. "I need to get some stuff from my locker."

He's never had a locker in his life. But he gets up anyway.

"Catch you later?" he says to me.

"Yeah," I say.

He is half way across the yard when he turns and waves at me. I wave back, and actually blush.

Loretta says, "Ah, now I get it."

"Get what?" I say.

"You like him," she says, as if she's just unravelled one of the great mysteries of time. "You're an item."

"Er, no," I say, and explain that Dylan and me have known each other forever and that we're really good friends but that's all. Because if Loretta likes Dylan, or if Dylan likes Loretta for that matter, there isn't anything I can say or do about it because it has nothing to do with me.

"Yeah right," she says, like she doesn't believe it for a minute. But what's not to believe?

Communication Breakdown
Led Zeppelin: John Bonham

Sam's school bag and shoes are lying in the middle of the hall. I put them away and go through to the living room where Dad is playing the guitar. He's wearing his fleece jacket over his Hawaiian shorts and a Led Zeppelin t-shirt and struggling over some chord progression; G minor, F, Eb – but he can't seem to find the fourth.

"Where's Sam?" I say, because if I am going to get a telling off, I would rather Sam weren't present.

"Upstairs?" says Dad, like, as if he's guessing. But he doesn't look up from his guitar. G minor, F, Eb... A minor

"Did anyone ring today?" I say. I want to know what Mr Badger said, and at the same time, I don't.

"Yeah," says Dad, trying more chords.

"And?"

G minor, F, Eb... D. "And what?"

"Who rang?"

"I don't know. I took it off the hook." G minor, F, Eb... D minor

"Oh!" I am a bit, like, floored by his answer. "Why did you do that?"

"Look, I was busy. All right? I'm trying to concentrate here and it's one thing after another..."

Maybe this isn't the best time.

I go into the kitchen and look for something to eat. The mouldy bread is still in the bread bin, so I throw it away and cut a slice of Sam's spare birthday cake to eat instead. Part of me is relieved Dad hasn't talked to Mr Badger, and part of me is bothered by it because it means I'll have to tell Dad myself.

When I finish my cake, I go back through to the living room. I take a deep breath and go for it. "Dad," I say.

G minor, F, Eb... C minor. He doesn't look up.

"Dad? Can I talk to you about school?"

Dad sighs and abandons his guitar. "I'm not getting anywhere with this anyway," he says. "What is it that's so urgent?"

"I got called into Mr Badger's office..." My throat is dry. I really wish I didn't have to tell Dad about this, but it's not as if it's going to go away."

"Colin Badger?" says Dad. "I used to go to school with him."

I know this already.

"He was one of those kids who did well at everything..."

I know this too.

"A bit like you..."

He's not making this easy for me.

"...I'm glad you haven't let me down."

It's a difficult thing to hear just before I tell Dad how actually I have let him down. Talk about bad timing.

The door flies open and Sam runs in doing aeroplane impressions, shooting me on the fly-by. He jumps on the sofa and turns the television on.

Dad laughs at Sam and shakes his head. "So what were we talking about?" he says.

"It doesn't matter."

63

Alone in my room, I pull out my homework diary to see what I need to do for tomorrow, but there's nothing urgent so I put on my iPod and try to forget my horrible day. Communication Breakdown, followed by Blink; Travis Barker on the drums. Travis had a horrible day once, a really horrible day. His plane crashed, people died and Travis was, like, seriously hurt. It puts my tiny troubles into perspective. What am I? A bit late for school? Not trying hard enough? Lacking concentration? If Travis can turn his life around, so can I.

I look at my kit and actually get as far as picking up my brushes. But what's the point? Even with the sound-off pads, Dad gets cross about the tapping and says it's like a death-watch beetle ticking away in his head. So instead, I sit down on my bed and kick ass on my imaginary drum kit. Crash crash crash crash, tom roll bass bass... through to the end. It's not the same. Travis hits the ride cymbal with the side of his stick to get a real brittle sound. You can't do that in thin air.

Back downstairs, Dad is watching adverts with Sam. Dad is glued; not to the products, but the background music. He likes to keep track of who is making money out of having their song sampled.

"Jammy," he says, when a really famous Dave Prince guitar riff is played behind a car insurance advert. "They could have used one of mine," he says. "Electric Summers would have worked. Just the right tone."

"Dad, they're not going to use your music for a car insurance ad, not with your record."

"My record?"

"Your driving record," I say.

Dad got banned from driving a year ago after speeding and then failing to stop at lights. Driving without due care and attention they called it and banned him for three years.

"Oh yeah," he says. "I forgot about that."

Mrs Pike has got this thing she says about people who forget their maths books and pens and stuff. It's 'you'd forget your head if it wasn't screwed on,' and I think of that now, because that's what Dad is like.

The phone rings.

"Who put that back?" says Dad.

Sam jumps up to answer, but I am scared it's Mr Badger so I grab Sam's arm to stop him and Sam squeals, like, as if I hurt him? I hardly touched him.

But Dad is all, "Leave Sam alone! Stop that noise! Pack it in the pair of you."

And Sam is all "Ow ow ow – she hurt me!" and whining.

So Dad leaps up to pull us apart and somehow the phone wire gets caught around his arm and the phone goes crashing to the floor.

Everything goes quiet. Sam and me just stare at the broken pieces of phone. Dad sits down. He is shaking. You can tell he's mad, but I don't know if he's mad at us for arguing or mad about the phone or what. Sam pulls a face at me; a kind of 'what do we do now' face. I go over to the phone to see if we can mend it, but it's broken into too many pieces.

Somewhere Else
Razorlight: Christian Smith-Pancorvo

I am standing in Mr Badger's office again. He says he has tried to phone Dad, but there's no answer. I tell him the phone has broken although judging from his raised eyebrows, I am sure he doesn't believe me.

"So I've written to him outlining my, or rather, the school's concerns," he says, and gives me an envelope addressed to Dad, with the school logo in the corner. "Will you please make sure he gets this tonight? I would like him to contact me tomorrow."

When I arrive in Biology they are discussing the brain and memory. Mr Mac tells me to sit down and join in when I am ready. I take out my exercise book and look at the white board where there is a diagram of the brain and two labels pointing at different bits; two types of memory - short term and long term. I try to concentrate but drift off, wondering how Dad will react to a letter from school when he thinks I'm doing okay. I wonder if he's bought a replacement phone, if he's even managed to get out of his pyjamas and if he's made any progress with his song. I don't want to think about Dad all the time, but he's like, got into the worry bit of my brain and it feels like he's staying there.

Mr Mac slams a book down on my desk, WHACK! "Daisy Meadows, are you actually listening and pretending not to, or are you in fact somewhere else in that happy little head of yours, completely ignoring the fact that this is a biology lesson and you need to pay attention?"

I wish the ground would open up and hide me forever. "I'm sorry," I say, sitting up straight to prove I'm listening now.

He continues. "So, there are some illnesses, where people suffer a loss of their short-term memory. Head injuries may cause temporary amnesia, and people with brain damage may lose their long-term memory altogether and even forget who they are, whilst retaining short-term memory. This shows us that different types of memory work in different ways…"

The rain is heavier than it has been all day, and noisy. It drums on the glass and sucks up my attention. Me and Sam will get soaked on the way home. We'll have to hang our wet clothes on the radiators if they're going to be dry enough to wear in the morning.

Mr Mac talks about repetition, stimulus and patterns. Drumming's all about patterns. I wonder which bit of memory I need to play American Idiot, Rock 'n Roll or Paranoid. In my head, I go there. Sit down, flex wrists, pick up sticks. Count; One, two, one two three four. Crash and snare and bass bass bass bass…

"So is everyone clear on that?" says Mr Mac. "Next lesson? A memory test. Come prepared. You have been warned."

I am most definitely not clear on anything. Everyone else is closing their books and I notice several people have drawn neat little diagrams and written notes. My book is empty, apart from Mr Badger's letter slipped between the pages.

She's All Right
Stereophonics: Javier Weyler

Dylan is sitting on the wall outside. Everyone else is rushing to get home out of the rain, but I guess Dylan is waiting for me. My heart starts beating, like, snare and bass bass, snare and bass bass. (It's the backbeat to Sunshine of Your Love and I know it's that because usually the snare gets played on the second and fourth, but Ginger Baker turned it round to play it on the first and third, putting the bass on two and four.)

I am such a geek.

Elaine, Dylan's mum, drives up in her VW camper van and the noisy phut-phut engine cuts out. Dylan jumps in. He doesn't even see me and I hate it that I am so bothered. Did I say bothered? No, I'm not bothered at all. The camper van door clunks shut, and I carry on walking.

The rain is pretty heavy, my hair is stuck to my face and there is water trickling down my back. Suddenly, an arm links into mine. It's Loretta. "Can I walk with you?" she says, slightly out of breath.

"If you walk fast," I say. I'm in a bad mood over nothing. And as soon as I say it I feel mean because Loretta's just being friendly. So I slow my pace. "Sorry. I'm not having a good day," I say, by way of explanation.

"You too? I broke a nail!" She shows me her handful of red nails including a broken index finger nail. "Never mind eh? Carousel will have to wait."

"Carousel?"

"This song what I'm learnin' on bass. It's Blink 182..."

"Oh I know who it's by," I say. "Awesome bass intro," because it is. Awesome.

Loretta's face breaks into a massive smile. "Totally amazo. That's what I'm learning. The intro." And she goes on to tell me how she's self taught on bass by watching YouTube videos of Mark Hoppus and Mark Hoppus wannabes.

I love that.

"We should totally get together," she says.

"Yeah, one day," I say. And I totally mean it too.

Wake Me Up When September Ends
Green Day: Tré Cool

Sam is wearing his Blackpool shirt with an old feather
boa from the dressing up box and Dad is wearing a top
hat, and a sparkly waistcoat with the buttons done up in
the wrong holes. They are telling each other jokes.

Dad says, "Why was the tractor magic?"

"Because it went down the road and turned into a
field," says Sam. "You always tell that joke."

"Okay," says Dad. "Well what about this one.
What's a snake's favourite subject?"

Sam thinks about it then shakes his head.

"Hisssssssssssstory," says Dad.

Sam giggles. "My turn," he says. "What's yellow
and dangerous?"

"I don't know," says Dad.

Sam says, "Shark infested custard," and giggles
some more.

"I know that one," says Dad.

"All right then, what's yellow and sings?" says Sam.

Dad thinks. "I don't know, what is yellow and
sings," he says.

"Lark infested custard," says Sam, which is actually
quite clever for a kid.

I clap, but Dad doesn't get it. "Larks are famous for
their singing," I say. But jokes are never funny if you
have to explain them.

"I've got another one," says Dad. "What's orange
and sounds like a carrot?"

"Do you mean a parrot?" says Sam. "Because if you do, the answer is a carrot."

"What?" says Dad, like, well confused.

"What's orange and sounds like a parrot?" says Sam. "The answer is a carrot! That's the joke."

"That's what I said," says Dad.

"No it's not," says Sam. "You said, what's orange and sounds like a carrot, but the joke is what's orange and sounds like a parrot? Carrots don't make sounds."

Dad shakes his head. "I don't get it," he says.

"Don't get what?" says Sam.

"Why a parrot would be orange."

At this, Sam actually falls over backwards laughing. He thinks Dad is being super silly. So I leave them to it and go up to my room.

I take Mr Badger's letter from my biology book and stare at the envelope. I know I should give it to Dad but I want to know what it says before I do. Carefully, I lift the flap on the back trying not to tear it. Downstairs Dad and Sam are giggling. As long as they are telling jokes I know I am safe to read, and pull the letter carefully from the envelope.

Dear Mr Meadows,

I would be grateful if you would contact the school to arrange a meeting with me, at your earliest convenience. As you may know, Daisy was involved in a fight this week, and whilst we would not ordinarily take action over disputes off school premises, this has caused us serious concern. We feel it is symptomatic of a general deterioration in Daisy's commitment to studies, her attitude and punctuality.

71

I would like to talk to you about how best to tackle these issues.
Yours Sincerely...

I get a sudden vision of Dad and Mr Badger together in school and it's horrible. There'll be Dad in his Led Zep t-shirt and Hawaiian shorts, and there'll be Mr Badger in a suit. And Dad will start talking about old times and how things were when they were at school, and Mr Badger will probably think the same as everyone else; that Dad's turned into a total nutter or something.

Why can't I just have a normal dad? I hate myself for thinking it, but sometimes I just wish I could slip into the background and never be noticed again.

Stuck in a Moment
U2: Larry Mullen Jr

It's late. Sam's in bed and Dad's playing the guitar in the living room. It's actually beginning to get on my nerves; same old chords over and over again, so I make myself some toast in the kitchen and drown Dad's noise out with my iPod music.

While I am eating, one of the pictures on the cork board catches my eye. It's Mum, and she's sitting at Ziggy's drum kit on a stage in Aberdeen. It's a picture I took with my Lego camera when Power of Now were touring the UK and Mum and me were allowed to go too. I was seven. It was the year before she got pregnant with Sam. Mum has dyed red hair, and a great big smile. She's not really playing the drums, but she looks so happy. Dad and Ziggy are stood either side of her, pulling funny faces and doing bunny ears, but Mum doesn't realise it.

There are pictures of Mum all around our house, in frames on the walls, in albums, and there's one I have in a locket in my room, but you stop seeing things which are there all the time; or at least you stop looking at them. For some reason, I can't stop looking at this picture of Mum. It's as if it's talking to me.

I take the photo off the cork board and stare at it.

I'm not staring at Dad, and I'm not staring at Ziggy.

I'm not even staring at Mum, not really. I'm staring at the memory of what was going through my head when I took that picture. It's a physical memory; a feeling. A feeling that even now twists something inside of me and opens a gaping hole I don't know how to fill.

I started banging on Ziggy's drums when I was three; had my own junior kit when I was four, and started proper lessons with Ziggy when I was six. By the time this picture was taken, I knew that whatever else happened in my life, playing drums had to be part of it.

Mum knew that too. Immediately after I'd photographed her, Mum called me over and said, "You're the one who should be in this seat. Not me."

I Miss You
Blink 182: Travis Barker

I was nine when Mum died.

And it was Ziggy who told me. Dad was still at the hospital with Sam, because he was in a special baby unit. I didn't see Dad and Sam for another week. Ziggy was cross with Dad about that. I remember him saying "You've got two children you know," down the phone, but Dad didn't come back until he could bring Sam.

Ziggy cried enough for both of us and said I was very brave, but I couldn't imagine Dad coming home without Mum. When he did, the time to cry had, well, kind of passed. I mean, there was Sam – this new little life to think about, and nothing else was real.

The next few months are jumbled and dark and serious in my head. There are things I remember; Sam's long eye lashes and the way he used to grip my finger with his tiny little hand. I remember being at Dylan's house a lot. I remember going out with Ziggy to buy drum bits from Mike. I remember Dad and Ziggy in meetings and arguing about the Power of Now and whether they should end it or not. And I remember Dad crying in the middle of the night when I was supposed to be asleep.

The first time I remember laughing, after Mum died, was Christmas. Sam was three months old. Dad said we had to make it a happy day because that's what Mum would have wanted. Uncle Ziggy brought a Christmas tree and I helped him decorate it with tinsel and fairy lights. When I woke up on Christmas morning, I had a pillow case filled with presents. The present I remember most was from Dad. It was a DVD of these two comedians called Morecambe and Wise. Dad and Ziggy used to watch them when they were boys and Dad said they were very funny. He said, "We need to laugh."

We pulled crackers with our dinner of chicken and roast potatoes, and I got ice cream for pudding. Dad and Ziggy had mince pies and beer. Sam had milk in a bottle wrapped in tinsel. And after dinner we watched the video.

Eric Morecambe, the tall one with glasses, was trying to play Grieg's Piano Concerto conducted by this famous conductor, Andre Previn. I'd never heard of Grieg or Andre Previn and until that day I didn't know who Morecambe and Wise were, but Dad and Ziggy literally cried with laughter, real tears and everything, and I guess it rubbed off on me too.

After that, we watched every Morecambe and Wise recording we could lay our hands on. Me, Dad and Ziggy.

Because You Loved Me
Power of Now: Ziggy Meadows

Sam appears in the doorway holding Martin; his pyjama trousers are wet and he's wiping tears from his eyes. "I peed my bed," he says. "And Daddy's asleep on the sofa."

"Bloody hell..." I say, but it makes him cry more. "No, no it's all right. Come here." I give him an arm's length hug. "Let's get you out of those wet pyjamas, eh?" I say.

Sam sees my wet face. "Are you crying too?"

I shrug, "Just having a silly moment."

"Why?"

I show him the picture of Mum, Dad and Ziggy.

Sam takes the photo from me and studies it. I can see from the movement of his eyes that he isn't just looking at Mum. And I can tell by the way he screws up his face that he is confused about something.

"Are you all right?" I say.

"Why don't we see Uncle Ziggy anymore?" he says.

"I don't know," I reply, which isn't entirely true. I mean, I know Dad and Ziggy fell out, and I know that for a long time Dad was real mad with Ziggy for abandoning us when we needed him most, but I can't understand why it's gone on so long.

Sam examines the photo and I find him some dry pyjama bottoms and a vest from the radiator. "You can sleep in my bed if you want." His little face lights up. "But you're not to pee in it..."

"Promise promise promise not to," he says.

I carry him upstairs and tuck my duvet around him so that he feels warm and cosy. He is still holding the photo.

"Is it my fault she died?" he says.

"Oh no, you must never think that. It was just one of those things that happen; no one's to blame."

"What was she like?"

I take the photo and tell him all about Mum; how her fingers were the longest fingers I ever saw, how she loved to sing and paint pictures and how she was a great runner. I tell him that she believed everyone should follow their dream. I tell him she would have loved it that he was a fast runner and he smiles. He has the same smile as her.

The same smile as me.

And then I pick out a book from his shelves and offer to read him a story. It's Mr Gum. I tell him, "It was Mum's favourite," because I want him to feel close to her. It seems so unfair that Sam never knew Mum.

He pulls Martin under the duvet with him and I read the story. It's always good to hear Sam giggle, and Mr. Gum makes us giggle together. After a while, Sam has trouble keeping his eyes open. I close the book and lie down with him, because I don't want to be on my own.

"Night night, Daisy," he mumbles, half asleep.

"Night night, Samster," I say.

From where I am, I can see the pictures on my bedroom wall. There's Cindy Blackman, Shelia E. and Carla Azur, alongside Travis, Bonzo and Keith Moon; my drummer Gods and Goddesses. Ziggy used to be there too. I don't remember taking him down, but he's not there now.

Wish You Were Here
Pink Floyd: Nick Mason

The last time I saw Ziggy was the night him and Dad argued, like, BIG time. Ziggy wanted to tour again, but Dad said he wasn't leaving me and Sam. Ziggy said we could tour with them. Dad said a tour bus wasn't the place for a baby. Ziggy said we could stay in hotels and get a baby sitter. Dad said he wasn't leaving us with strangers. Ziggy talked about wasting potential and opportunities. Dad said he wasn't wasting anything and he was perfectly happy living at home with his two kids…

It went on like that for days.

And then on this particular night I was lying in bed and their quarrel woke me up. I heard shouting and the front door slamming, and it scared me.

I crept downstairs expecting to see Dad, but it was Ziggy sitting there alone. "What's the matter, Kid?" he said.

"I'm afraid of the dark," I said, because I didn't want him to know I'd heard them fighting.

He opened his arms for me to go and sit with him.

After a while he said, "There's nothing scary about the dark." He wrapped his jumper around my shoulders and said, "Come on, let me show you something."

We went out into the garden where we sat on the old wooden bench. It was autumn. There was a chill in the air and it felt crisp and fresh.

"What are we doing out here?" I said.

"Just look at that!" he said, pointing up at the cloudless night sky. "Isn't it beautiful?"

"It's dark," I said.

"You're not looking, Kid. There's about a million billion stars out there. A million billion little tiny suns."

"So?"

"So how can it be dark when there's all that sunlight out there?"

I looked up at the silvery specks sprinkling the universe like magic dust.

"They're no different to the sunshine what wakes you in the morning, what warms you when you're cold, or the sunshine what puts a smile on your face just because it's there. Sunshine's never far away," said Ziggy. "It just depends on where you look and what you're looking for, Kid."

We held hands then, and looked up at the sky again, at the darkness and the trillions and zillions of little tiny suns. I didn't feel scared any more.

"This is what I call a Zen moment," said Ziggy.

"What's a Zen?" I said.

He tried to explain it to me. "Zen is about being complete; it's about being whole. Mind, body and spirit in harmony and at peace; perfect and without conflict or contradiction."

I didn't get it. I didn't even know what I didn't get. But Ziggy was really calm and still, and I felt safe and protected just being with him. Not just then, but always.

"This moment," said Ziggy, eventually. "It's all there is. All that stuff in the past, and everything you don't even know about yet, none of that's real."

I wanted to believe him, because in that moment I was happy. Nothing else mattered. The jumper had fallen to the ground, but I wasn't even cold. The air smelled fresh and the only sounds were far away. When I looked around I saw tiny droplets of dew on the grass and the plants, sparkling in the starlight. It was the most beautiful thing I had ever seen. I felt calm and peaceful and I wasn't scared anymore.

"I like it here," I said. "Can we stay up all night?"

"We'll stay up as long as we're feeling the vibe, Kid," said Ziggy.

So we sat there, me and Ziggy in the middle of the night, not talking, not thinking, just being still.

I don't know how long it was. I snuggled up close to him and felt my eye lids getting heavy. I rested my head on his shoulder. I felt him breathing and I heard him whisper, "This moment is all there is. It's all there will ever be. Just this moment. That's it. And in this moment everything is possible..."

Next day he left, and I haven't seen him since.

I used to ask Dad where Ziggy was and when we would see him again, but every time I did, Dad looked angry and refused to talk about it. In the end I gave up asking, although I never stopped wondering.

Good Times Bad Times
Led Zeppelin: John Bonham

There are noises in the street; bin men. I sit up.

"Where's my clock?" I say, remembering that I forgot to set the alarm.

Sam picks it up from the floor on the other side of the bed. "It's ten past seven," he says, rubbing his eyes and yawning as if he has all the time in the world.

I grab the clock and see that he doesn't. "Look! We need to hurry." It's actually ten past eight. I jump out of bed and am first into the bathroom. I wash and dress quickly and fly downstairs to find Dad sitting at the kitchen table, wearing his joggers, a shirt and a tie. He's drinking tea with the teabag still in the mug. Yeuch.

"Why didn't you wake me?" I say.

Dad looks at the clock. "Is that the time? Sorry, is there anything I can do?"

I shove two slices of bread in the toaster and pour two glasses of milk. "You could shout at Sam," I say. "Tell him to hurry." And then I put some biscuits, cheese and fruit into our lunch boxes while Dad meanders towards the door.

Sam skips into the kitchen before Dad leaves. He is wearing an old Iron Maidens t-shirt of mine and says, "Ta daa." The Iron Maidens are, like, the world's only female Iron Maiden tribute band. I know he will get crucified for wearing it, but he's going to have to find that out for himself. We don't have time for a show-down.

I spread the popped-up toast with jam and give Sam one slice. "We'll eat on the way," I tell him. We grab our lunchboxes and schoolbags while Dad looks on. He just doesn't seem to get the urgency.

I arrive at school late, again, and Mrs Pike finally cracks. "Daisy Meadows. I've had it with being patient," she says. "After school detention. Today. DO NOT be late."

At lunchtime I make it to our seat. Dylan is alone, and when I call his name he turns, smiles and pats the space next to him.

"Where have you been?" he says. "I've been ringing you but I just get the engaged signal."

I explain about our telephone breaking, and ask him why he rushed off with his mum last night.

"Badger phoned her," he says. "About the fight." He touches the bruise on his nose. "She said I wasn't allowed out for a year!"

"She's joking, right?"

"She wasn't when she said it, but she's probably forgotten by now. So if you want to walk my way tonight, we could walk together."

I tell him about my detention.

"Are you okay?" he says.

And I'm suddenly aware that he's looking at me, I mean, right at me. "Yes. Why?"

"Because you don't look like you're okay," says Dylan. "You look really fed up."

"I'm fine," I say, but it comes out wrong and sounds snappy, because I'm tired and hate the thought of staying late when I could be walking home with Dylan, having a laugh. And then we sit in silence. One minute we are friends connected by years and experiences, and the next minute we are separate beings with nothing to talk about.

"Daisy," he says, after a while. "Don't take this the wrong way, but you just seem different. Less um… relaxed? Less… happy?" He pauses to think. "Less you," he says.

I don't answer him straight away because he's struck a bum note which resonates loud and clear. I can ignore it from Mr Badger and Ebony and I can even deny it to myself, but when Dylan says I've changed, there's a kind of ringing in my ears that won't go away. He's talking about the drum business, although he doesn't know it. Or rather, the lack of drum business. And in my head, I'm like, a drummer – a drumkit = a what?

I don't know the answer.

Maybe if I was Carla Azur, Rick Allen or Travis Barker I could work it out, because they had to live without drumming too, except they got it back. One way or another, they all got back their voice. Me, I just don't know what to say.

Of all people, I owe Dylan an explanation. "Meet me later?" I say. "I'll tell you everything then."

"Okay," says Dylan. His brown eyes look sad. I know he cares about me and I know I'm lucky to have him as my friend. "Come to my house. Whenever you're ready."

In detention I look around at my fellow inmates. They are the usual suspects; Watson's meat-head pals, the part-timers, the petty criminals. They jeer when someone new walks in, and tip back in their chairs, unbothered by requests to be quiet, sit properly and behave. They are the regular school mess-ups. And I don't belong here. I promise myself, as soon as I sort out this thing with Mr Badger, I'll get my head down, concentrate in lessons and do all my homework. It'll be, like, turning over a new leaf; starting a whole new page in the book of Daisy Meadows, and all these things I've done, they'll be in the past.

When the bell rings I see Mr Badger lurking outside the door. I take ages to pack my chair away hoping he will disappear, but I can't hide forever.

"Ah, Daisy," he says when I leave the hall. "Your father hasn't rung yet, I'm afraid."

"I know," I say, and remind him about the broken phone. "I'm sure he will."

Mr Badger sighs. "Please do, because I really would like to speak with him."

Thunderstruck
AC/DC: Chris Slade

Dad and Sam are playing a game. It's called Hunt the Slipper. Dad used to play it with me when I was a kid. It involves one person hiding a slipper or shoe somewhere in the house, and the other person looking for it. It's Sam's turn to look and he is, like literally, turning the house upside down to find Dad's manky footwear and loving every minute of it. Dad won't give him any clues either.

I enjoy watching them play together and it reminds me of when I didn't find Dad so embarrassing and annoying.

Sam eventually finds the slipper hidden behind Dad's guitar and he's dead pleased with himself, high-fiving me and strutting around the room. Then he tells Dad to close his eyes while he hides the slipper. Dad does as he's told and Sam buries it under the cushion next to Dad. Dad opens his eyes and looks in cupboards, behind the sofa, in the rubbish bin and then goes out of the room to look in other places. Sam is high. He's thinking he's really fooled Dad and he's going to win, but it's so obvious Dad is just stringing the game out to keep him happy.

But when Dad returns he is carrying a menu for the Blue Lagoon, our favourite takeaway. "I think we'll get Chinese for tea," he says. "What do you want?"

"You haven't even found the slipper yet," says Sam.

Dad does this sort of what are you talking about look and then says, "Oh yes, of course. Well give me a clue."

"You didn't give me any clues," says Sam.

"Didn't I?" says Dad.

He looks at me for help. I like, nod towards the sofa and Dad goes over and feels between the cushions.

When he pulls out the slipper, Sam says, "That's not fair. Daisy told you!"

"It doesn't matter, Sam," I say. "It's only a game."

But Sam is obviously tired and storms off to his room in a sulk.

Dad hands me the creased and dog-eared menu which surely must be out of date by now, and I choose something for me and Sam to eat. He'll come down as soon as the food arrives.

I sit by the window watching the lightning, waiting for the thunder and tracing the rain drops with my fingers. Dad is taking ages and I can't go to Dylan's until he's home. Even if there is a queue, getting a takeaway wouldn't take this long. Would it? I start finger drumming on the windowsill; paradiddles with a flam on the first note – flamadiddles; LRLRR RLRLL – starting slow and getting faster. And I'm wondering how all this will end; the school stuff, the drum stuff and whatever stuff it is that's making me so badly want to see Dylan.

Sam comes down from his room and wants to know, "Where's Dad?"

I tell him Dad will be back in a minute because I don't want him to worry, and I suggest we play Hunt the Slipper again, just us two, to pass the time.

Sam has first turn at hiding Dad's slipper. I carry on looking out of the window, and see in the reflection Sam hiding the slipper behind his back, under his jumper.

"Ready!" he shouts.

I make a big deal out of looking, just like Dad did, and Sam is, like, "This is so hard. You'll never ever find it. Not in a zillion billion trillion squillion years." At least he has cheered up again.

"Give me a clue," I say.

"You have to sit on it," says Sam, which is just the most misleading clue in the history of the world, and I have to stop myself from complaining or he'll know I know.

Instead, I look on shelves, behind Dad's guitar, in drawers, and behind the curtain. And when I do, I see Dad walking up the path. It's a massive relief.

"I give in!" I say to Sam. "Dad's here with tea. You win."

Sam slaps my hand with a victory high-five, pulls the slipper free of his jumper and races to the door to let Dad in. I go into the kitchen to get plates and forks ready.

Sam walks into the kitchen holding Dad's dripping wet hand. Neither of them is carrying food and then I see Dad's face. Underneath the wet hair sticking to his skin, I can see a bruise on his forehead and a cut on his bottom lip. There is watery blood trickling down his chin and onto his shirt.

"Oh my god, what happened?" I say.

"I fell over," says Dad.

"Are you okay?"

"Yes, I'm fine," he says.

"But what did you do?" It's hard to imagine what kind of fall could have caused Dad to damage his face like that.

"I think I must have fainted," he says.

"Where?"

"In town," he says.

"Where in town? Had you already been to the Chinese?"

"Chinese?"

"The takeaway?" I remind him.

"Oh, um, no," says Dad.

"Didn't anyone help you?" I say. Thinking about Dad lying there, on the pavement in the rain, bleeding, makes me feel really sad. I sit him down and get some kitchen towel to clean up his face.

"Yeah, um... that bloke with the face... um, you know the one?" says Dad.

"A bloke with a face?" I say. "Well that certainly narrows it down a bit." I'm trying to make a joke, and thankfully Dad laughs.

"What am I like?" he says.

Sam gets Dad a towel and wraps it around his shoulders. I wonder out loud about taking Dad to the hospital but he is adamant he doesn't need to go. He has hated hospitals and doctors ever since Sam was born. "It's just a bruise," says Dad.

Outside, the thunder and lightning are right overhead. I can't go to Dylan's in this, but to be honest, I don't feel like leaving Dad and Sam anyway.

Life Less Frightening
Rise Against: Brandon Barnes

Mr Badger is lurking again. When he sees me, he noticeably quickens his step in my direction. I dig in my bag, pretending I am looking for something, but he's still heading my way. So I turn around and bump into Loretta coming out of the music block. I link my arm into hers and say, "Hide me! I don't want him to see me."

Loretta catches on quick. She sees Mr Badger too and we start walking, no - marching away from him. Hopefully Mr Badger will find it too much like hard work to catch us.

"Daisy!" he says, loudly.

I am mega embarrassed and wish that vaporising into thin air were humanly possible.

"Daisy!" he calls, louder.

We stop walking and I look at Loretta. "Sorry," she whispers. "Not fast enough."

"I'm still waiting for your father," says Mr Badger, catching us up. He does that thing with his thumb and little finger, as if he is miming 'phone me'.

I can practically feel Loretta's jaw drop next to me, but she doesn't say anything. "Yes, I'm sure my dad will ring soon," I say.

"I sincerely hope so!" he says, hurrying away to catch up with another wayward pupil.

I feel sick inside. He's going to speak to Dad one way or another and then on top of all my other crimes, they'll both want to know why I didn't give Dad the letter and why I keep lying to my head-teacher. I'm not even sure myself anymore.

Loretta and I watch him bounce across the yard to tell off some year sevens for kicking a ball too close to windows, and then Loretta says "What the eff?"

I turn to face her. "Please don't ask," I say.

She holds up her hands and replies, "Okay, I won't. But just so's you know, I'm here if you need a friend, Girl."

I wonder if she knows how good it feels to hear someone say that.

When the Levee Breaks
Led Zeppelin: John Bonham

When I get home, Dad is wearing his pyjamas and Led Zep T-shirt with the Hawaiian shorts over the top, and he's watching some crappy quiz show.

"Where's Sam?" I say, because it's his first night at Beavers and I've bought him a good luck card. He's never done anything like Beavers before and I know he is really excited, but nervous too.

"Not sure," says Dad, not even looking at me.

"The longest river in the UK is…" says the TV presenter. Dad bangs the side of his head with his hand, trying to jog his memory.

"The Severn," I say. "220 miles."

"I knew that," he says to me, then shouts, "THE SEVERN!" at the TV.

"Is he in his room?" I say.

"I don't think so," says Dad.

"And for a further ten points, the longest river in the World is…"

"Oooo, I know that one," says Dad. "Don't tell me."

"The Nile," I say, on my way out of the room. I run upstairs and poke my head into Sam's bedroom. He's not there. So I open the bathroom door and am immediately hit by a wall of steam. "Sam?" The hot tap is running and when I step inside I tread in a puddle. The bath is overflowing. No sign of Sam. "Daaaaad!" I shout, turning off the tap, pulling the plug and grabbing towels to mop the floor with. I swear under my breath.

"Longest river in the world – now in our bathroom. Hoo-ray."

Dad arrives at the door. "Oh my goodness," he says. "I was going to have a bath wasn't I? I'm sorry. I just got involved in Cash for Questions. Let me help." He grabs some more towels from the airing cupboard and starts mopping too.

"Did you actually collect Sam," I say, not for a minute believing he didn't.

Dad hits his head. "OH SHIT!" he cries. "No..."

"What?"

"Sorry, sorry, I'll go now."

"No, I'll go. You clean this up." I don't see why I should clear up Dad's mess, and anyway, I'll be quicker.

I run the route Sam and I would normally take, wondering if school will let him out without Dad being there. I half expect to see him any second and half expect him to be sat in Miss Magick's class steaming at the ears. But the further I go, the more anxious I get. An ambulance blue-lights past me on Highgate and I get a horrible feeling. Kids get run over all the time. Sam might be one of those kids. What if a kid was knocked unconscious and he didn't have any ID on him and the people at the hospital couldn't get in touch with his relatives? How would that kid feel, thinking he'd been abandoned? What if he died? If anything happens to Sam I... I... I'll never be happy again.

My chest grips at my lungs and heart and it feels almost too hard to breathe, but I start to run. With every step I repeat in my head, *Sam's safe, Sam's safe, Sam's safe*. I don't want to let myself think anything else.

At the top of Finkle Street, I see Alex and Curtis Watson with a group of other boys. Panting and with my chest aching, I stop to get breath. All I can think about is how empty my life would be if Sam wasn't in it. He's my kid brother and he's a pain sometimes, but I love him. I lean forward, resting with my hands on my knees and head down. "Sam's safe," I say out loud, to chase away the horrid empty thoughts.

And when I look up, there he is.

Sam. Safe.

But he's walking real slow and dragging his school bag behind him; no blood, no ambulances, no big crowd around his lifeless little body… just Sam. I shout his name.

He lifts his head to reveal puffy red eyes, and calls "Daisy!" then runs to me and wraps his arms around my middle.

"What's the matter?"

"Daddy never came to get me and I waited and waited and then I lied about seeing him so they had to let me go."

"It's okay," I say. "You're safe and that's the only thing that matters."

But Sam is still upset. "Curtis Watson was mean to me today because his dad saw our dad getting thrown out of the Chinese takeaway. And then he wouldn't let me play football cos I was wearing a girl's t-shirt yesterday so I kicked him, and he told, and I got done for kicking and Miss Magick had to go early and I don't like Mrs Grimes, and I didn't want to go home because I've got a naughty letter for Daddy…" Tears streak the dirt on his face and snot bubbles from his nose.

"Oh poor Samster," I say, giving him a used tissue from my pocket. "Let's just get you home, eh?"

Sam wipes his eyes and his sobs turn into sniffs. "What about the letter?" he says. "I'll get done won't I?"

"No, you'll be all right. I'll sort it." I would do anything for Sam.

He puts his cold hand into mine and squeezes. I squeeze back, then pick up his bag, swing it over my shoulder and together we walk up Finkle Street. There are still kids from school hanging about in town, although I can't see the Watsons anymore.

It starts to drizzle and we walk quicker.

After a while, Sam says, "Do you think Dad really did get thrown out of the Chinese?"

"Of course not," I say. "That's just something stupid Curtis made up to upset you."

"I didn't believe it anyway," says Sam.

At home, Sam and I strip off our soaking wet coats and jumpers in the hallway. I am surprised when Dad doesn't come to see us and apologise.

"Look at this," he calls instead. "There's a four hundred year old stone bridge been swept away by a river swollen with rainwater. Four hundred years! And now it's gone. Just like that…"

"Sam's here," I call. "I found him on Finkle Street."

We go through and Dad looks up from the TV. He sees Sammy's red puffy eyes and immediately jumps up. "Sam! What's the matter?"

"You forgot me!" he says.

Dad's eyes dart between me and Sam and there's a flicker of horror on Dad's face. "Oh Sam. Oh Sam. Oh Sam…. I am so sorry. What am I like? Can you forgive me?" You can tell Dad is really cut up about it. He opens his arms to Sam. "Aww, come and sit with me

Sammy. Just remember, I. Am. A. Numpty. What am I?"

Sam giggles. "A numpty?"

"Yeah!" says Dad. "I am a numpty."

Upstairs, I get changed, grab a dressing gown and Martin the Kangaroo for Sam, and pick up the wet towels from the bathroom flood, then go back downstairs. I give Sam his things, take the wet stuff through to the kitchen and put it in the washing machine. Then I sit down to read Sam's naughty letter, except it isn't about Sam's behaviour; just something to do with the school uniform swap shop. And there's no way Sam is going to wear uniform anyway, so I throw the letter in the paper recycling wishing that all letters were as easy to bin. I make eggy noodles with peas for tea, and take it through so that we can eat on our laps.

After tea, Dad picks up his guitar and Sam gets ready for Beavers. I give Sam his good luck card and he kisses me on the cheek.

"Are you taking him?" I say to Dad.

"Where?" says Dad.

I take a deep breath before I answer. "Beavers. Like, it's Sam's first night, remember?"

Sam looks at me. He's not impressed that Dad has forgotten something as big as this; he's been looking forward to Beavers for almost a year. "Will you take me, Daisy?" he says.

"Of course I will, Sam. It'll be a pleasure!" I say the last bit really pointedly in Dad's direction, but it washes over him. So I ask Dad if he has some cash to pay Sam's subs.

And Dad says, "Yeah, take whatever's in my wallet." He starts strumming on his guitar; one of the first songs he ever wrote. It's beautiful and everything, and I love to hear him play, but it would be nice if he didn't leave everything to me.

"Where is it?"

Dad looks around, as if he's looking for the wallet and then says, "Where's what?"

I snap. "Your wallet? Sam needs subs, remember?"

But Dad just shakes his head. He doesn't remember. He doesn't remember anything because he doesn't listen. And it's really beginning to get on my nerves.

"Help me, Sam?"

We look everywhere. Sam checks the fridge but it's not there. I go upstairs and check Dad's chest of drawers, and then Sam shouts, "Found it!"

The wallet is in the paper recycling bin, under the school uniform letter and the Blue Lagoon menu. I take out some coins and give them to Sam, who runs off to get his shoes on.

"I'm going to put this in your coat pocket," I say to Dad. "Will you remember?"

"What?" he says, plucking at his guitar strings.

"Will you pay attention?" I say. "I'm putting your wallet in your coat pocket."

"Okay. Thanks. Got it."

Honestly, it's like dealing with a six year old. No, it's worse, because at least Sam listens. I go into the hall where Dad's coat is hanging and drop the wallet in his pocket, except that there's something in the way and it won't drop down. When I put my hand in to remove the blockage, I find another Blue Lagoon takeaway menu; a different menu with a new design and more choices.

I get a funny feeling inside. A new menu + Dad's bruised face = ??? I don't like what I am thinking.

"Ready!" says Sam. He's got his shoes and his monkey hat on.

I stuff the menu back in Dad's pocket because I can't let Sam know the Watsons might have been right. "Do you really need to wear that?" I say.

He grabs the sides of the hat, pulls it tight down over his ears and gives me a glare.

I'm not going to argue. "Come on then. Let's run," I say. "Or we're going to get soaked."

Losing Touch
Killers: Ronnie Vannucci

There are things we need to come clean about. Dad needs to tell me what really happened at the Blue Lagoon, and I need to tell him about Mr Badger's letter. And on the way back from Beavers, I try to think of the best way to bring it up without getting into an argument.

I still don't know what I'm going to say when I get home, but as I open the front door, I can hear Dad singing.

"Half a lifetime torn away
And I'm breaking more with every day
I've had good times, and bad times
And I wish I had the key
To turn back time and find that piece of me..."

He once told me it was a song about Mum and I stop to listen, to hear if it is finished. He sees me in the doorway, and says, "What are you doing, sneaking around like that?"

"Sorry," I say. "I didn't want to interrupt your flow."

"Chance would be a fine thing," says Dad. "There's a bloody great big wall in the way and no way around. Listen." He plays the verse through, one more time and stops. "What comes next?"

"Beats me," I say. "You're the song writer."

So he goes back to the guitar, and repeats the same chords, over and over again. He doesn't get any more, and gives up. "Did you want something?" he snaps, abandoning his song and reaching for the TV remote.

"Cup of tea?" I suggest, buying some time.

In the kitchen I make tea, grab some biscuits and the Blue Lagoon menu, and return to the living room. Dad's watching a programme about the coastline of Britain. It's a repeat, but Dad doesn't care. He takes the tea without looking at me.

"Sorry I snapped," he says. "I just get so mad. You know, I used to be able to write a new song every week, and I've been working on this one for a few months now. What's holding me up eh?"

I shrug. "Writer's block?" I say, trying to sound like I understand.

He sips the tea and takes a biscuit. "You want Chinese?" he says.

"No, I don't want Chinese," I say.

Dad frowns, and points at the Blue Lagoon menu. "What's that for then?"

"I'm not trying to catch you out," I say. "It's just last night you went out for takeaway, and you came home with cuts and bruises instead. You said you never got to the Chinese."

Dad's eyes narrow and he's nodding.

"But I found this in your pocket…"

"So?"

"So you must have reached the Chinese to get this; it's a new menu. The old one's in the recycling."

"Does it matter?" says Dad.

"Well… like… yes," I say. "Because I know you're forgetful sometimes, but forgetting where you've been

100

and forgetting how you got bruises on your face are a bit different to forgetting where you left your wallet..."

Dad thinks about this for a minute, then hits the side of his head. "What the hell is going on in here?"

I feel sorry for him. I put my hand on his arm to stop him beating himself up any more and say, "Dad, I'm worried about you."

"Well don't be," he says. "I'm fine." He shoves a whole biscuit in his mouth and dips another one in his tea. He might not want to talk about it, but I need to.

I take a deep breath and say, "Alex Watson reckons his dad saw you in there..."

"You know," he says, thoughtfully. "You might be right. I did get to the Chinese... because now you say that, I remember going through the door and Barry Watson was there... Oh that's right. Of course."

I'm like, relieved he remembers, but it's not the whole story. "What happened then? Because you didn't come home with food."

There's a far away look on his face, as if he's piecing together some jigsaw memory.

I sip my tea.

His face screws up. "No," he says, shaking his head.

"Okay, well do you remember when you came home last night? And you said you'd fallen over and I asked if anyone had helped you?"

Dad nods, but even so, I'm not convinced he does.

"You said a man with a face had helped you."

Dad laughs.

I laugh too because it sounds so ridiculous. "Do you remember who he was? Do you remember anything about him, other than that he had a face?"

Dad is giggling and cannot answer. His giggle is infectious and I laugh too, but I'm also really frustrated.

Nothing ÷ anything = nothing.

I can't get him to tell me what happened and, like literally, throw my hands up in the air, grit my teeth and mime a scream.

"Why are you pulling that face?" says Dad.

"Because …" I say. "Because I just wish you'd remember things occasionally. Because it's driving me mad when you don't!"

"So I'm a bit forgetful," he says. "It's not your problem."

"But don't you see? You make it my problem when the bath water overflows or you forget where things are or forget what you're doing in the middle of doing it! Have you any idea how hard it is living with someone as disorganised as you?"

And the thing is, Dad looks, like, totally bewildered. So although I want to have the discussion, the argument, call it whatever you like, I can't; because Dad's not playing. He looks at me as if I am nuts, then turns to watch a man on TV talk about the chalky cliffs and the view over to Calais. He doesn't answer me, and I don't know if he's trying to think of something to say in his defence or if he's just turned me off.

When he starts channel hopping, I guess I've got my answer. End of.

Things You Discover on a Cold Dark Night
Power of Now: Ziggy Meadows

I leave the house early and call in at the Chinese on my way to get Sam. The girl behind the counter is called Penny. She used to go to my school, and she played piano. She was really good – not my kind of music – but I still liked listening to her play.

She knows who I am too and when she looks up from her book and sees it's me, she says, "Is your dad okay? That Watson guy; he's such a dork."

I ask her to tell me what happened exactly.

She says, "He had a go at your dad about that competition at Mike's. Talk about holding a grudge; it was months ago."

"What did he say?"

"He said you'd cheated because there was no way a girl could drum better than his boy. Your dad made out as if he didn't know what he was talking about, and that really wound up Dork Brains. I had to ask them to leave. It was upsetting for other customers. I don't know what happened after that. Is he okay?"

"He bust his lip and banged his head. Says he fell over, but he can't remember."

"Head injuries can do that," she says. "You should take him to a doctor."

Penny is, like, sympathetic and wishes Dad well and all that, but she has said all she's going to say about

Dad and Barry Watson. Other customers are arriving and she has a job to do.

Outside Beavers, parents wait for their kids. Mike is one of them because he's got a kid a year or two older than Sam.

"I heard about Elvis last night. Is he all right?" he says.

"What did you hear?" I say.

"About his fight with Baz Watson."

"His fight? Do you know what happened? I mean, exactly?"

"Don't know how it started but they were shouting at each other on Highgate when Watson jumped him; just laid into him. Tommy Wilson saw it..." Tommy Wilson has a strawberry birth mark on his face; it's very distinctive. "... He pulled them apart and sent Watson off with a flea in his ear. Your dad insisted he was all right. Was he?"

"Yeah," I say. "Just a couple of bruises."

"That's good. Give him my regards, yeah?"

I nod. Does knowing this make any more sense than not knowing? I can't decide. And we stand around awkwardly while Mike talks about my win in the competition and how he hopes I'm going to enter again and how he's got some new stock in the shop including some beautiful black Mapex kits and if I'm interested he will do me a decent discount... Basically it's more of a monologue than a conversation and I am rescued by a swarm of boys in turquoise sweatshirts with painted faces, running out of the scout hut.

Sam comes out carrying a junk model of something that appears to be a giant pepper pot. "Look what I made!" he says. You can tell he's really proud of it.

"That's er… really nice," I say.

Mike says, "Is that the Ulverston Lighthouse? It's grand that, Lad."

Sam beams, so I know Mike is right, but honestly it could be the Eiffel Tower for all I know.

And then Mike's kid comes running over to us and barges into Mike, almost knocking him over. Mike laughs, and whilst holding his kid at arms length, says (in this matter of fact normal everyday voice), "Is Ziggy still in Ulverston?"

"Ziggy's in Ulverston?" I say, like, shocked.

"Last I heard he was," says Mike. But his kid is hyperactive or something, punching Mike in the legs, dipping into his pockets and fiddling with his iPhone. "Leave that alone!" he says to the kid.

I want to ask him more, but he's already chasing the runaway boy, trying to get his phone back.

Memory
Sugarcult: Kenny Livingstone

Sam rushes in ahead of me with his toilet roll model.

"Look what I made!" he shouts. "It's the lighthouse in Ulverston. Can we go and see it? Dan's been inside! Can we go inside?"

Dad says, "Oh yes, very nice, Sam."

"Can we go?"

"Yes, whatever."

So Sam says, "Can we see Uncle Ziggy too?" I wasn't even aware of Sam listening to my conversation with Mike, and here he is, daring to say the very same words I was planning to say.

"Ziggy?" says Dad. "Why? Where is he?"

"Ulverston," says Sam. "Mike said."

Dad looks into thin air and he's obviously racking his brains to jog some memory, and then repeats, "Ulverston? Ulverston? Are you sure?"

"What actually happened was that Mike asked if Ziggy was still in Ulverston," I explain.

Dad looks back into space, and after a while he shakes his head. "I don't know where he is," he says. And then adds, "Ulverston's only down the road."

I probably have about a hundred questions I want to ask Dad now that the subject of Ziggy is no longer taboo, but the one which fights its way to the front of the queue is, "Didn't you know he was there?"

"Yeah, don't you like Ziggy?" says Sam.

Maybe Sam's question is easier to answer than mine, because that's the one Dad answers. "Course I like him," he says. "He's my brother."

"Then why don't you know where he is?" says Sam. "Daisy knows where I am."

Dad says, "You live in the same house. It's different when you grow up. You have different lives. You want different things." He gets up and pulls a CD from the rack. It's the platinum selling CD - Simple Truths. Dad looks fondly at the cover…

POWER of NOW
SIMPLE TRUTHS

Dad and Ziggy are in their twenties. They stand back to back, long hair, shirtless, and tanned. They look moody. Ziggy is hugging his drumsticks; Dad is hugging his Fender Strat.

…and passes it to Sam. "That's us," he says. There's a sparkle in his eyes and warmth in the tone of his voice which I wouldn't have expected. "When we were kids, we had the best fun swapping identities; just clothes and toys when we were little, but when we got older we swapped classes at school, and did each other's tests and wrote essays for each other; that kind of thing. It's like having a best friend, only better."

I know they did all that because they've both told me before.

"Did you argue?" says Sam.

"Not really," says Dad. "Sometimes I used to think he was a bit jealous because I won writing prizes and music competitions, but Ziggy was good at things too. He was brilliant at maths and he had more energy than me. And he chose the name of the band." Dad chuckles to himself. "We did argue about that. I said it was a lousy name and wouldn't last. He said it was timeless. Turned out he was right eh?" He laughs a big belly laugh like I haven't heard in months, and stares at the CD cover shaking his head and smiling. "We changed the bass player three times before this," he says. "Gave up in the end and hired session players for recordings and gigs."

"No," says Sam. "I mean, did you argue when you were grown up? Is that why we don't see him any more?"

Dad's eyes seem to cloud over and he shakes his head. "Yes, I guess we did. Stupid, isn't it? We got very angry with each other, and Ziggy left. I didn't know where he'd gone... where did you say he was?"

"Ulverston," I remind him.

"Yeah, Ulverston. I wonder if he's still there." His face looks drawn and grey "Promise me something," he says, looking at both Sam and me. "Promise me you'll never be pig-headed and stubborn and fall out like your dad and uncle."

He's not angry anymore, just sad.

With a Little Help from my Friends
Beatles: Ringo Starr

Because it's Saturday I am having a legal lie in. I've been awake for a while but since everyone else is still in bed, I don't need to get up. My iPod's on shuffle and I'm just relaxing with my music.

Until Sam bangs on my door. "Someone's here! Someone's here!" he shouts, and bursts in. "Someone's at the door!"

"So answer it!" I say.

He rushes downstairs. I turn off my music, pull a sweatshirt over my pyjamas and follow.

Dylan and Loretta are standing in the doorway, together. Sam is looking at Loretta. "Who are you?" he says.

Dylan says, "Thish ish Mish Moneypenny. And I'm Bond. James Bond. Licenshed to kill." He cups his hands into a gun shape, fires an imaginary bullet and blows the smoke from his fingers.

Sam copies with his own cupped hands and giggles.

"Who on earth is it?" calls Dad, from upstairs.

Sam skips off to report on the visitors, repeating "Thish ish Mish Moneypenny," over and over again.

I look down at my pyjamas. Dylan and Loretta are both dressed for rain. For a second, or maybe two, I consider not inviting them in, but I'm kind of bored with having no friends. "Come in," I say, even if it is going to be embarrassing.

In the kitchen, I set about cleaning up last night's dinner mess. Without a word, Loretta runs a basin of soapy water and puts the dishes in. I clear the table and wipe the work surfaces and Dylan starts on the washing up.

"Thank you," I say. "I'm not used to help."

While we all muck in with the washing up, drying and putting away, Dylan starts to explain how him and Loretta just bumped into each other.

"Yeah," says Loretta, taking over. "I was on my way to buy strings for my bass because you know that song I was playing? Carousel? Well I've reached the end of the intro even without my best nail, but now I need new strings because the old ones are mega dirty. I've had 'em years, and the sound is über dull and totally dead…" She stops to think for a second. "Oh Em Gee! Unless it's me what's dull and dead!" she says, throwing her head back to laugh.

"I'm sure you're really good," I say.

Loretta smiles at Dylan, then turns to me and says, "I'm well happy you think that because Dylan's just invited me to be in your band. Is that okay with you, cos I'm totally smashed about it?" She looks sooo excited.

It takes me by surprise. It shouldn't, because I did sort of agree to the band thing. I just didn't think Dylan would go ahead and arrange things without me. "Um, I suppose so." I say. "But…"

"Who are we gonna be like? I mean, cos there's only three of us. Blink obs. Nirvana? The Manics? We could practise in school, if that's a prob. I mean, otherwise it'll have to be here because I don't have a drum kit and I'm guessing Dylan don't either. What are your

110

neighbours like about noise or have you got them muffler thingys what dead the sound…"

"No!" I say, louder than I intend.

Loretta stops talking. There's an awkward silence. Her and Dylan look at each other, and it's obvious they have been talking about me.

"My neighbours are the least of my problems," I say.

"Is it Badger?" says Dylan. He stares at me, waiting for an answer. I love it that his eyes are so brown, and almost perfectly symmetrical. "Well?" he says.

I shut the kitchen door so I can talk in private and finally tell Dylan and Loretta about how the teachers think I'm messing up at school and that I haven't even told Dad about Mr Badger's letter. It's such a relief to get it out in the open.

"Why didn't you give your dad the letter?" asks Dylan.

I shrug. "Because I didn't want to upset him I suppose and I know it's stupid, but the longer I left it, the harder it was to give it to him."

Loretta says, "That head bloke doesn't look like he's gonna give up though, does he? You'll have to tell your dad sooner or later."

"I know."

"But when we is famous, right, with our band, you'll laugh about all this. You will. You'll look back and think, what was I stressing about?"

I love Loretta's polished gloss on my problems and I wish it was all as simple as just getting over a bit of stress. I didn't realise it before but everything is linked; the way Dad is behaving, the reason I am failing at school, the possibility that this might not go away. And something is beginning to take shape in my mind.

"Listen," I say. "There's something else I haven't told you."

They wait for me to explain, while I search for the words which will make sense of everything.

"I'm not playing drums anymore," I say, eventually. "The noise of me practising was too much for Dad. He got upset every time I played and it was just better to stop."

Dylan cannot believe it. "Is that why you're not doing music?"

I nod. "I know what you're thinking. It was dumb. But I was, like, trying to make a point; a stupid point which was completely wasted... I'll take it up again one day... He won't be like this forever..." I say, but trail off because a horrible thought drifts through my mind.

"Aren't you doing any music at all?" Dylan looks shocked and reaches across the table to shelter my hands inside his own. Loretta sits down next to me.

I talk about the shopping trips, the sour milk, the flooded bathroom, the way Dad can't remember how to do basic things sometimes and how embarrassing he has become in public, but I don't tell them about his forgotten trip to the Blue Lagoon because just thinking about it makes me feel sick. "I'm scared," I say. And as the words come out, I realise that fear is a feeling I've been holding back for some time now. Dad's forgetfulness, his disorganisation, his lack of concentration; they're getting worse, not better.

After a while, Loretta says, "Do you think he's depressed?"

And Dylan says, "If there's anything we can do to help, just say."

The weird bit is, just talking to someone has already helped.

"I really appreciate you being here, Guys," I say. But there's still that dark thought lurking in my mind, and I'm not sure I want to say it out loud. Except, what have I got to lose? "Thing is," I say, without looking up. "What if he keeps getting worse? What if it's not depression and he's got something really wrong with him? What will happen to me and Sam?"

It's a question nobody can answer.

Success Story
The Who: Keith Moon

Sam comes shopping with me. We have the list and get round the supermarket in record time. I make sure we remember bread and Sam makes sure we remember bubble bath. And because we finish so quickly, we decide to treat ourselves to a custard doughnut and milkshake in the café, which makes him extra happy.

There are free magazines to read in a pile next to the counter and Sam grabs a comic for himself and a Cosmopolitan for me. I have no intention of reading it, but Sam is rapt by The World of Disney and I am left with nothing better to do than flick through anti-aging advice and frank discussions about modern relationships. It's totally tedious and I hope I never end up enjoying a magazine like this. But then something does catch my eye. It's an article entitled 'Famous Band Reunions' and includes references to the reunions of:

Blink 182

Rage against the Machine

Blur

Faith No More

Limp Bizkit

The Who

Led Zeppelin (who did a charity concert in 2007 with John Bonham's son standing in for him)

and most recently, Stone Roses.

It makes me think of Dad and Ziggy; well, the splitting up part. But then I get this crazy idea in my head.

"Why are you smiling?" says Sam.

"Never you mind," I say. This has to be done properly and I can't have Sam messing it up. I tear the page out of the magazine, fold it carefully and put it in my pocket.

Revelations
Iron Maiden: Nicko McBrain

After tea, I tell Sam he can have his bubble bath. He jumps off the settee and runs upstairs. By the time I have caught him he has tipped the entire bottle into the running bath water. He strips off, climbs in and within minutes he is clapping at the massive foam mountain, making bubbles fly everywhere. He asks for some plastic animals in the water, and he wants Martin to sit on the toilet and watch him play. I tell him he can have whatever he wants as long as he doesn't flood the floor.

Downstairs, Dad is watching TV.

"Is this a good time to talk?" I ask. I want to show him the article from Cosmopolitan. I turn off the TV and sit down.

"Ooh, this looks serious," he says. "You're not going to tell me off are you?"

I try not to be irritated by Dad's attempts to be funny, and say, "No. But I've had an idea." I show him the article, and watch his face for a response, but there's nothing. It's as if he's wearing a mask.

We hear Sam upstairs, singing a song about kangaroos.

Dad gives me back the article. "Why are you showing me this?"

"I'm showing you because it made me think of you and Ziggy."

He laughs and says, "I have no idea why."

"Because when we were talking about Ziggy yesterday," I say, "You looked sad that you don't know where he is."

"Did I?"

"Yes, and I know the band split up because you had me and Sam to look after, and I know Ziggy wanted to carry on gigging…"

"What are you saying?"

"Well, me and Sam are older now. And I just thought, wouldn't it be amazing if we could find Ziggy … and you got back together… like all those other bands." I point to the Cosmo article. "You could have a Power of Now reunion."

Dad shakes his head. "I don't know where Ziggy is."

"No, but we could find him. How hard can it be? We know he was in Ulverston."

Dad looks straight into my eyes as if he is, like, totally freaked out. "No way!" he says.

I get that sick in the stomach feeling again. "Yes way," I say. "Mike said he went to Ulverston. We discussed this last night."

But Dad doesn't reply. He is searching his brain, trying to remember or something. And he does that banging thing, with his hand on the side of his head. "Ulverston? But that's just down the road."

It's horrible. We both know there is something wrong, but I don't want to be the one to say it and I guess he doesn't either. So we sit in silence, listening to the ticking of the clock, Sam singing to Martin, and the rain on the window. I notice things I wouldn't normally; like a pile of unopened letters on the desk, the Power of Now platinum disc hanging on a slant, the stubble on Dad's chin which is more like a beard every day, and how his fingernails need cutting.

I want to be somewhere else, not saying what I am about to say.

Sam calls from the bath. "Shall I wash my hair?"

But I have to say it. I have to find the courage to say what needs to be said. So I imagine Dylan is here with me, holding my hand and urging me to speak. I take a breath, and then from somewhere inside me a little voice is freed. "Dad, do you think it's worth seeing a Doctor?"

"Daisy! Shall I wash my hair?" repeats Sam.

"No…" says Dad, to me. "Not for a bit of forgetfulness."

"I'm washing it anyway," shouts Sam.

I don't answer Sam and Dad doesn't say anything else. He reaches for the TV remote and turns on some programme about archaeology.

"Dad, I'm serious. I'd like you to see a doctor."

"And I'm serious too," he says. "I don't need one. I'm short on sleep and a bit forgetful. Not ill."

And that's it. He's not going to change his mind so there's no point in trying to make him. And maybe I am blowing a bit of forgetfulness out of proportion. I don't understand how he can remember stuff about his childhood and yet not remember a conversation we had yesterday, but what do I know?

While we sit and watch Time Team piecing together some ancient's life it all goes round and round in my head, like a never ending loop. Worried, scared, confused. Worried, scared, confused. Worried, scared, confused… I feel myself getting more and more wound up. Honestly, if I don't get out of here, I'll explode.

I'm Lost Without You
Blink 182: Travis Barker

I grab my iPod and my jacket and walk out of the house without even bothering to say goodbye. It is raining, and almost dark. At Abbot Hall Park, I stop and watch a gang of kids, younger than me, messing about on the zip-wire and an old guy walking a fat yellow dog round the path. Apart from them and Tom DeLonge singing in my ears, I am alone. I want to be alone, but I've still got that crowded out feeling. So I keep walking; across the river onto Aynam Road.

At the zebra crossing, a VW van stops to let me cross and I think it might be Elaine's van except I don't want her to see me upset so I don't look. And instead, I run over the road and up Parr Street and keep running till I get to the bridge over the old canal. It's a cycle path now, but you can still see the grooves in the wall where the tow ropes have left their mark; a memory of how things used to be.

I walk through Fletcher Park, past the horse chestnuts and the beech trees, past the cemetery and up the muddy path to the castle at the top of the hill. I don't care about the rain or the mud or anything; it's just good to be up here breathing in huge lungfuls of fresh wet air, above the world.

When I was at Dale Primary, we had a trip to the castle and they told us Catherine Parr used to live here. She was one of Henry the Eighth's wives - the last one - which meant she outlived him.   Divorced beheaded

119

died divorced beheaded survived. We learnt that at Dale too, but it's only any good if you can remember which order the wives are in. They've since discovered that Catherine Parr never lived in Kendal and everything has been named after her and Henry for nothing. After the event, years later, it's just not possible to know what the real truth is. I don't know why, but that makes me think of Dad and Ziggy.

I wish things were different between them and that Ziggy had never gone away, because if Ziggy was here, I could talk to him. Even if there isn't some big band reunion concert, I still want to see him. I could tell him about Dad and school and Dylan, and he'd let me play the drums at his house and …

… And my life would be so different.

I look up at the sky, hoping to see the billions of tiny little suns, but all I can see are clouds and the dark. Ziggy's voice comes into my head. "Sunshine's never far away," he says. "It just depends on where you look and what you're looking for, Kid."

I might not be able to see the distance right now, but even in the dark I can still make out the river and the Town Hall, the old snuff factory, K Village, the astro-turf lights, school and everything. I can hear the traffic and when the wind drops I hear the sounds from the ski slope. The rush of air on my face sort of clears my head and stops me thinking. I love it up here, and away from home I feel whole again.

Seize the Day
Avenged Sevenfold: The Rev (James Owen Sullivan RIP)

When I get home, Sam is draped in a wet towel watching TV. The heating has gone off, he has goose pimples on his arms and his lips are blue. He isn't talking to me because I left him in the bath and the water went cold before he finished washing his hair. Dad says he's told Sam to go to bed, but Sam is refusing. There is an upside down waste paper basket on the floor, and a carpet covered in litter.

But I am calm. The walk and the fresh air have done me some good, and I can deal with this. I get some pyjamas out of the clean washing and tell Sam to put them on.

Sam looks at Dad, with that sticky out angry jaw and says, "You forgot."

"I'm sorry, Sam," says Dad.

"What does he mean?" I say, to Dad.

It's Sam who answers. "I told him the water was cold and he said he'd bring me up a kettle. But he forgot." He says that last word, *forgot*, with real venom. He's mad all right, but it isn't worth arguing.

"How about we make it up to you with some hot chocolate and a story?" I say. "We could do that couldn't we, Dad?"

Dad says, "How about it, Sam?"

Sam doesn't answer.

"Well?" I say.

"Just you reading a story," he says, looking at me. "Come up in five minutes."

Dad shrugs it off. He said sorry, after all. I plonk down on the sofa, and kick off my dirty shoes. I don't even care anymore about the mud on the carpet. It'll be me who clears it up.

A woman on the TV says, "...And welcome to the new series of Family Meltdown. Tonight, our celebrity family is put to the test to raise money for charity, and have a bit of fun at the same time ..."

"Are you all right?" says Dad.

I say, "Shall you make the hot chocolate or shall I?"

"Our family will be putting themselves through some extreeeme challenges..." says the woman.

"I'll make it," says Dad.

"Whether it's white water rafting, walking on thin ice or wading through crocodile infested swamps, we're focused on fun..."

"And I know what you're thinking," says Dad.

"Do you?" I say.

"But I forgot the hot water because I found something. After you said that about Ziggy, I went and looked in my old diaries."

"You keep a diary?" I never knew.

"Not any more. But I did when I was younger and they're all in a box under my bed. So I went to look at them and there's a whole pile of stuff I'd forgotten about." He stops, like, to think or something. "Including a letter."

"Who from?"

Dad pushes a creased envelope across the coffee table towards me. "Read it. "

I take the letter. There is a cartoon picture on the envelope of Dave Grohl playing drums; big white teeth, giant smile and a sweaty head of hair flying all over the place. 'Nirvana' is scrawled across the bass drum. It's a letter from Ziggy.

Quietly, Dad says, "I don't even know if I replied." He is clearly upset. "I'll make that drink," he says, and leaves me alone with the letter.

I stare at Dave Grohl. It is treasure; almost too precious to open. Ziggy was, is, an excellent cartoonist. He used to have this scribble pad with dozens of pictures he'd drawn of people. They were always very funny, with their nose or lips or something drawn really big and comical to make the person look ridiculous.

Dad returns with the hot chocolate and I haven't even opened the letter. Sam is calling me, so I put the envelope in my pocket and go up to see him with the mug of hot chocolate.

He is wearing my old princess pyjamas.

"I'm sorry I went out and left you," I say. "I just needed some fresh air."

"I don't mind you going out," he says. "But I do mind cold water baths. And Dad said he'd get me a kettle and when he didn't I had to use cold water to rinse my hair. Why does he forget everything?"

"He doesn't forget everything," I say, trying to sound reassuring. "He remembered your birthday, didn't he?"

Sam nods.

"And he remembered you like kangaroos, and that you like chips and he got those balloons."

"And he remembered about when he was six," said Sam. "He told me." He is smiling now. "He told me that him and Ziggy both got bikes and that his was red with silver wheels and Ziggy's was blue with silver wheels and they both had bells with Batman on. He said

123

Batman was different when he was a boy, not scary like he is now."

"There you go," I say. "He's just a bit forgetful. And everybody forgets things. It doesn't mean he's a bad person or a rubbish dad."

"He's the only dad in the whole school who's ever been on TV."

I put my arm around Sam. He's a sweet kid really.

"Daisy," he says. "He will be all right, won't he?"

"What do you mean?"

"I mean, sometimes when he forgets things I am scared."

"What are you scared of?" I say.

"Like, when he didn't bring me the hot water, I was scared he'd fallen over with it or something and got boiled alive. Because he doesn't just forget does he? He does other stuff, like he gets muddled and he's always dropping things. Why does he do that?"

"I don't know, Sam," I say. "But I'm sure there's nothing to worry about. Maybe he's a bit tired. He's not sleeping very well is he?"

"Are we going to live happily ever after?" says Sam.

I smile. He's thinking of fairy tales and it isn't fair to pretend life's like that. Real life isn't always happy and unless you actually die, it's not even about ever-afters. Nothing lasts forever.

"So?" says Sam. "Will we all live happily ever after?"

"You can destroy your now by worrying about tomorrow," I say, thinking out loud.

"What does that mean?"

"It means, let's not worry about living happily ever after; let's just be happy now. It's what this amazing singer called Janis Joplin once said.

"Is she happy now?" says Sam.

"Yeah," I lie. I can't tell him she's dead.

Sam looks at me. He nods and his face breaks out into a big sunshine smile. "I love you, Daisy," he says.

"And I love you too, Samster," I say.

When Sam is settled, I want to be alone again. I hide in the bathroom away from him and Dad, and read Ziggy's letter.

Honey Pot Cottage,
Coniston Way,
Ulverston.

Elvis,
I know you're mad and you see this as some kind of betrayal, but it's not like that. Throughout our lives you've been the one who shakes and moves everything. You got Power of Now up and running and if it wasn't for you, I'd still be serving lentil burgers to vegetarians in some wholefood café somewhere or selling my cartoons to tourists. And I'm grateful for every opportunity you ever gave me – not just being in a band, but being in the BEST band ever, touring the World, sharing your family with me. I've loved every minute of your life.

But the single thing that keeps ME going is playing. I'd have followed you to the end of the Earth if I could have played drums all the way there. When circumstances pulled the plug on that dream, I started to lose myself.

What do I do if I don't drum? Who am I? Why don't I feel connected? I can hear your voice now; 'You're an uncle, a brother, a member of this family.' And

Man, believe me when I say those things mean a lot. It's just that they're all on the outside of me and I need to find what's within. This is my spiritual journey, Elvis. I don't know where it will take me, but you've got to let me look. Please don't go all stubborn on me, Dude.

The ball's in your court now. Write back, soon.

Zigs

Fireworks
Power of Now: Ziggy Meadows

After a night of little sleep, I'm lying in bed, listening to one of Dad and Ziggy's songs. It's the one with the most totally amazing drum solo in the middle because it helps me feel close to Ziggy. My hands are itching to pick up the sticks and join in, but even though I can't, listening to this explosion of everything that's great about rock drumming makes me smile.

When you first learn, you just want to play as fast and as loud as you can. There I was, thinking what mattered was how many fills I could do, or how fast I could roll on the tom, or whether my hi-hat was getting enough play. And there was Ziggy saying, "Play the music, not the drums. Ain't nothing wrong with simple, Kid; you can play a simple back-beat with heart, and it's just as enjoyable as the complex stuff," which is kind of ironic considering what I'm listening to.

But Ziggy was a good teacher and a great player. You only get to be that good if you know what you're talking about, and he tried everything he could think of to stop me overplaying.

"Focus on the individual beat. Everything before and everything after is just distraction. The beat is the only thing that matters."

He sat down and showed me. "Listen," he'd say. And there we were, one beat at a time, listening to the quality of each sound, the depth, the vibration, the silence. And gradually the beats got closer together.

"Keep in the groove, play time and feel inside the music," he'd say, picking up the pace. "It's not all about the pyrotechnics." And after a while, I started to get it. Drumming isn't about the HOW, as much as the WHY and the NOW.

I pull Ziggy's letter out from under my pillow and read it through again and again, and every time, the final line leaps out at me. *"The ball's in your court now."* Dad's words last night make it painful reading. *"I don't even know if I replied."*

Just as I return the letter to its envelope, the doorbell sounds; a continuous finger pressing riiiiinnnnnggggg.

"Can't someone else get it?" I moan, as I climb out of bed, put on my slippers and sweatshirt and go downstairs. I am still holding the envelope.

I poke my head into the living room. Sam is jumping up and down on the settee screaming at some sort of Sunday morning kids' game show on TV. Dad must still be in bed.

"Someone's at the door," says Sam, not looking at me.

"So why don't you answer it?" I say

"Sorry!" he says, still jumping and, like, literally screaming with laughter.

I open the door. And I don't know what I expect, but it is the nicest surprise. "Dylan!"

He smiles and tips his head slightly to one side. "Are you all right?" he says. "Mum saw you on Aynam Road last night and she said you looked upset. I thought you might have been coming to see me, but you never showed up."

We laugh, a bit awkward and embarrassed maybe, and I invite him into the kitchen where we can be alone.

128

I offer him cereal, but he's already eaten breakfast, so I make some tea and we sit down, on opposite sides of the table. Dylan's hands are both wrapped firmly around his mug, while mine fiddle with grains of spilled sugar. Underneath the table our feet bump together then quickly find their own space again.

"Were you?" he says.

"Was I what?"

"Upset."

"Kind of," I say. "But I think I'm all right now."

"You think?"

"Dad and me had a bit of a falling out over ... well, stuff. I needed to get some fresh air and space, that's all. When I'd calmed down, I got home and Dad had found a letter from Ziggy." I give Dylan the envelope. "You can read it if you like."

Dylan laughs at the Dave Grohl cartoon and pulls out the letter.

When he's read it, I say, "I'm going to find him, starting there." I point to the address in Ulverston.

Dylan softly touches my hand and says, "Can I help you?"

I am suddenly conscious of the way Dylan's fingers stroke my fingers and dance on my skin, on the back of my hand, on my arm. I am conscious that this feels like more than just friendship.

"I would love you to," I say.

Bring Me to Life
Evanescence: Josh Freese

I've left a big note on the fridge for Dad. It says –

DAD – REMEMBER TO COLLECT SAM

And after dropping Sam I go straight to the bus station, where Dylan is waiting. He pecks me gently on the cheek and then tells me he's lied to Elaine about needing to be in school early. I feel bad he is bunking off, but kind of special at the same time because he is lying to be with me.

Dad knows I am going to look for Ziggy, but he doesn't know I am missing school to do it.

On the bus, Dylan and I look out of the windows and make small talk for a while, about school, teachers and meat-heads. We sit next to each other, legs and arms touching, his honey smell brushing onto me. Then Dylan says, "I'm serious about a band. And I've thought it all through. We move your kit to my house so we won't upset Elvis with the noise, and you can come round and practise anytime..."

It's like, probably the sweetest and kindest thing anyone has ever offered to do for me.

"...And we should definitely enter Battle of the Bands."

He has woken some feeling inside me; made the impossible seem real for a few seconds. But as lovely as Dylan's offer is, I can't leave Dad and Sam together after school while I'm off practising and having fun. As painful as it is to say no to Dylan, I must. "I'm sorry. I just don't think I can commit right now. Why don't you find another drummer?" At least he can still live his dream.

Dylan shakes his head. "It's not going to happen. You're the only drummer for me, and without you there is no band."

So Far Away
Avenged Sevenfold: Mike Portnoy

We get off the bus in the middle of Ulverston.

"Where to?" says Dylan.

I pull Ziggy's letter from my pocket and read, "Honey Pot Cottage, Coniston Way."

We ask a shopkeeper if he knows where Coniston Way is, and he gets out a map and writes down the route on a piece of paper. It takes us about fifteen minutes because Coniston Way is a little outside Ulverston, near the Monastery. I have butterflies in my stomach and don't want to talk, but being with Dylan and not saying anything feels all right.

We turn into Coniston Way and see Honey Pot Cottage immediately. It is the only house in the street. The garden is wild and the house is covered in a yellow rambling rose, with brown tinged flowers. We walk up the path, and knock on the door. I know the likelihood of Ziggy answering is about a million to one, but still I hope.

A man answers the door. He looks much older than Dad, has less hair and a very lined face. He is dressed in a kind of long, dark red robe with trousers underneath. He nods with his eyes. "Can I help you?" he says. His voice is soft and somehow welcoming.

"I'm looking for someone. I have this address for him. He's my uncle. Ziggy Meadows," I say.

The man smiles, a big remembering smile. "Ah, come in," he says, and stands back to show us into his cottage. I can't believe it's this easy. I grab hold of Dylan's hand just to make sure I am not dreaming.

There is no hallway and we are straight into the living room. The first thing I notice is the sweet flowery aroma. The next thing I notice is the noise; or lack of noise. Like, it's totally silent; no radio, no TV, no music. Dad would love it. And then I notice a little table with a statue of Buddha, candles and incense holder. There is a little bell-in-a-box at Buddha's right knee, and a supply of incense at his left. There are fresh cut flowers from the wild garden and apples and oranges in bowls, and some black and brown striped stone beads coiled up neatly in front of Buddha.

No drum kit. No evidence of Ziggy.

"Please sit down," says the man.

There are several low, cushioned seats around the edge of the room. The floor is bare wood, apart from a rug in the middle. Dylan and I sit on the seats. The man sits crossed legged on a mat below the large garden window. I keep looking at the door, expecting Ziggy to walk in.

The man nods at us. He says, "I am Guishan Soko. I remember your uncle very well."

"You remember him?" I say. My heart, literally, dives and crashes into pieces. "You mean he's not here now?"

Guishan Soko shakes his head and looks down at the ground.

"But when did he leave?" I ask, desperately clutching straws and hoping it was, like, this morning.

"Several years ago," says Guishan Soko.

I feel like curling up in a ball and crying. He could be anywhere by now.

"What was he doing here?" says Dylan.

"Your uncle wanted the answer to a question."

"What do you mean?" I say.

"Your uncle's question was, why am I not fulfilled? Many people ask the same question but the answer is not the same for everyone."

This isn't what I expected. I feel out of my depth and look to Dylan for support. I know he understands what I am feeling and thinking.

"Why did he ask you that?" says Dylan to Guishan Soko.

"A long time ago he came to some seminars I gave in Kendal. He was always keen to pursue his understanding of the practise of Zen and Buddhism, but the time was not right for him. I believe he toured the world, playing drums in a rock group."

I nod. "The Power of Now."

Guishan Soko smiles at this. "He came to me after the group had stopped performing. He already had a great understanding of the theory of Zen, but he desired help to practise it himself. We worked together for several weeks before he came here to stay."

"What did you do?" says Dylan.

"I encouraged your uncle to observe his mind, to observe his thoughts as if from the outside. When he did this, he experienced... gaps, in his thinking. And during these, gaps, he was able to feel at peace with himself. He wanted to explore this in greater depth, so he came to stay with me."

"He wrote to my dad," I say. "I haven't seen him for about four years. This is the last address I have for him."

"I remember him writing to your father. When he didn't receive a reply, he was angry; upset. He knew he needed to let those feelings go. Buddha tells us, we are shaped by our thoughts; we become what we think. When the mind is pure, joy follows like a shadow that never leaves. Your uncle did not like what he was becoming. So he moved on. He wanted purity; to find Zen through his drumming."

"I'm sorry," Dylan says, "But isn't meditation about being peaceful and quiet?"

Guishan Soko cups his hands together and nods his head gently. "Let the activity be not the means to an end, but an end in itself. To find a sense of presence in the now is to lose ones self in what one is doing. Your uncle's joy was drumming."

I know what Guishan Soko is talking about. It's what Ziggy tried to teach me when he taught me to drum. It all makes perfect sense even though I can see Dylan is struggling here. It explains why Ziggy went away and why he wanted Dad to contact him. It doesn't however, explain where Ziggy is now.

"Don't you have any idea where Ziggy might be?" I ask.

"I'm sorry," says Guishan Soko. "But no."

We walk back up the path and into Ulverston in total silence. When we get onto the bus I am thankful I don't have to do the journey alone. We look out of the windows at the sea on one side and the Lakeland fells on the other.

It is drizzling again and everything is grey.

Complicated
Avril Lavigne Band: Josh Freese

I haven't slept much all night; partly because I was thinking about Ziggy and wondering how I am going to find him without clues, and partly because Dad was playing the guitar.

So I am tired; black bags under the eyes, grumpy don't-talk-to-me-or-I'll-bite-your-head-off kind of tired. And Sam has locked himself in the bathroom and I need a pee and if he doesn't come out soon I'll wet myself. Like, I am actually serious.

I knock and knock and beg and plead and eventually Sam appears with his hair all wet and flopping over to one side of his head. I push past him and sit on the loo.

When I come out, Sam is in my room. "What are you doing in here?"

"I'm looking for hair gel," he says, as if it's the most natural thing in the world to be rooting around your older sister's things.

"Well get out! I don't have any."

"You used to have some," says Sam, ignoring my demand.

I grab his arm and march him towards the door. "No. I've never had hair gel," I lie. "Now get out."

"Ooo!" says Sam. "Mrs Miserable Head."

I push him over the threshold, shut the door and I lean against it with my arms folded while he tries to open it again. "Ha!" I say.

When he stops pushing and I am quite convinced he's gone, I get dressed for school.

By the time I get downstairs, Sam is having an argument with Dad. Clearly, I am not the only one to have had a bad night.

Sam is wearing the monkey hat and Dad is complaining that it's too small. "Will you buy him a new one," says Dad, to me.

"Me? Why don't you?"

"Because…"

"Because?" I say, a bit too loud.

"Because…" Dad bashes the side of his head, and screws up his face. He's obviously frustrated, but so am I.

"Because he's your son?"

"Okay okay," says Dad, "I was only asking."

And I know I'm being a grump, but I can't help myself.

When I get to King's, Mr Badger is policing the corridors and when he sees me he is straight on my case. "Where were you yesterday? I was expecting a call from your father."

I tell Mr Badger I have been ill and say that Dad was preoccupied looking after me.

I think he is going to give me real grief over this, but instead he says, "Well I *am* going to speak to your father. I've gone ahead and arranged a meeting on Friday. I expect him to attend. This letter explains everything." He pushes an envelope marked PRIVATE AND CONFIDENTIAL into my hands. "Unless I hear otherwise, I will See. Him. Then."

I go straight to registration, sit at the back and open the letter. It's pretty much the same as the last one except there is an extra bit about the meeting, "...to discuss Daisy's behaviour, attitude and motivation." He wants Dad and me to be there, and someone called Miss Kelly (an Educational Welfare Officer) and Mrs Pike are also invited.

When everyone goes off to class, Mrs Pike keeps me back. "You're not to worry about the meeting," she says. "I'm going to be there, and everyone wants the best for you. You know I'm on your side. If you want to talk anything through before the meeting, come and see me. Yes?" Mrs Pike is kind and gentle and makes me want to tell her everything. But even though I want to, I don't.

The rest of the morning is a nightmare. I can't concentrate for thinking; about the meeting, the whereabouts of Ziggy, Dad's forgetfulness, Dylan and drumming; or rather – not drumming. I get a discipline slip in English for not handing in homework I didn't even know I had and get snide remarks from Watson about a certain someone getting kicked out the Blue Lagoon.

At lunchtime, Dylan is waiting on our seat.

"Look, I got us this," he says, digging in his bag for something. "It's the last day to sign up, so I put our names down." He hands me a piece of paper. "Just in case. And if we can't do it, then ..."

"What is it?"

"Our official entry into the Battle of the Bands."
I look down at the paper in my hand. It has a time and a date; the end of half term, which is just a few weeks away. "You know I can't do this," I say.

"But things might have changed by then. And we need you," says Dylan.

138

"Have you listened to anything I've told you?" I say, and screw up the entry confirmation and drop it on the floor.

Dylan stops smiling. "What did you do that for?"

I shouldn't have to explain to Dylan. Of all people, he should know why this is impossible. People are looking at us and I see them snigger and whisper. Dylan bends down to pick up the piece of paper, and you know what? I can't be bothered anymore. Not with school or people or competitions. I've had enough.

I walk across the yard, down the front path and out of school. Dylan calls me, but he doesn't follow. Just as well; because I want to be on my own.

I walk to Gooseholme and plonk myself on the seat where Dylan and I fed the birds. Looking at the water helps me to calm down. A heron flies across the field and lands on the stones in the middle of the river. I watch, waiting for it to make a move. I think about how beautiful and graceful herons are when they are standing and how ugly and prehistoric they look in flight. And I stay perfectly still, watching the heron, wondering if it can see me, and thinking how simple a heron's life is – just flying, fishing, nesting. I watch … and breathe… not thinking, not feeling, just being.

And I don't know how long I am like this, because it's as if this moment lasts forever.

No future.

No past.

Just me, as I am. Now …

… When the heron takes off suddenly, I have an idea.

Following the River
The Rolling Stones: Charlie Watts

Dinnet is this tiny village in Scotland somewhere between Aberdeen and Glasgow. It's next to a small loch and surrounded by trees and hills and it has a café, a pub, a handful of houses and nothing else. We stopped there in the tour bus, the day after the Power of Now Aberdeen gig because Ziggy was starving. It was a blue-sky-sun-shiny day so we bought egg sandwiches and crisps and juice in the pub and sat on the grass outside. The landlord was very friendly and he told us there was a beautiful walk around the loch and we should take advantage of it while the weather was good.

It was a good few miles, so half way around we stopped for a rest. We saw a deer in the distance, and a heron fishing. Ziggy lay back in the heather and said he was in heaven. He said that one day he would run away from it all and live there. When got back on the bus, Dad and Ziggy told each other bad drummer jokes all the way across the mountains and Ziggy laughed and joined in; that's how good a day it was.

I remember it so clearly now. If Ziggy wanted to be at peace with himself, that is where he would have gone. I wonder if I could get to Dinnet on my own. I don't even know where it is, exactly, but I am sure it's where Ziggy will be.

I walk along the Waterside thinking about seeing him again and how amazing it would be. Maybe it would lift Dad out of his depression or whatever it is he's got. And I play with idea of Power of Now doing a come back tour and me and Sam going along for the ride! As I get to the end of the Waterside, it occurs to me that even if I can't get to Dinnet in person, there may be another way to find out if Ziggy went there.

I go straight to the library on Stricklandgate and log on to a computer. I don't know exactly what I'm looking for – just hoping for inspiration – and type Dinnet into Google. It comes up with all sorts of tourist information and accommodation sites about Royal Deeside. I find something about the Loch Kinord Walk in Dinnet too, which must be the same walk we did. Half way down the third page are images of Dinnet, including one of the pub where we had lunch.

I click to enlarge and click again to go through to the website. There is a phone number right next to the picture. My heart beats in quintuplets. I write down the number on a leaflet about library opening hours, close down the computer and leave.

Don't get too excited, I remind myself. It's just a guess. He might not be there. He might never have gone there.

Outside in the rain, I look at the number. It's the only number I have and it's, like, a needle in a haystack, but it's worth a try.

The nearest phone box is next to Gooseholme. I put in my money and dial the number of the pub. The phone rings three times and someone answers.

"Alice Macdonald, Dinnet Hotel. Can I help you?"

My mouth is dry. I realise I haven't a clue what I am going to say and she might not tell me even if she does know Ziggy. Maybe she might even say she doesn't know him and then go and warn him someone is looking for him. I could make things worse here…

"Hello-oo," says Alice Macdonald, again. "Hello, can you hear me?"

"Yes," I say. "Hello. Um… I don't know if you can help me, but…" I stop. What do I say? How do I ask?

"Well let me try, Dearie," she says. "Fire away."

"I'm looking for my uncle. I think he might be in Dinnet. We came up there about eight years ago and had sandwiches in the pub, which is why I've phoned you." It sounds utterly ridiculous. I'm holding the phone with my right hand and all four fingers on my left hand have crossed themselves.

"Well I wasn't here eight years ago, Dearie. But I can ask around…"

"No, wait," I say. "He hasn't been gone eight years. If he's been there again, it will have been in the last four years."

"What's your uncle's name?"

"Ziggy," I say. "Ziggy Meadows."

There is a silence then, during which a million thoughts rush through my mind, but Alice Macdonald's voice interrupts them and says, "THE Ziggy Meadows? The drummer?"

"Yes," I say.

"Och I know him all right. The whole of Aberdeenshire knows Ziggy."

And I can't believe what I'm hearing. I feel a rush of pure excitement and I want to shout and laugh and cry all at the same time. But I manage to contain myself. Maybe she only knows him because he's famous. "Do you know him personally?" I say.

"Och yes," says Alice Macdonald. "He was here about a year, right enough. Had a little croft across the river and banged his drums all day and all night; and I don't just mean in the literal sense. No, Lass, he taught a whole bunch of our youngsters how to play and was quite the Mr Popular."

"So where did he go?" I ask.

"Travelling," she says. "Him and Anna wanted…"

"Anna?" I say.

"Aye, his young Lassie. They went off to see the world before…"

Beeeeeeeeep…. The phone goes dead.

"Hello? Hello?" I say, even though it's obviously pointless. I press the buttons, knowing full well it won't burst back into life and all I get is the dialling tone. I realise I've run out of change.

I hang up and go to the sweet shop. I buy a tiny bag of sweets, flying saucers, so I can get as much change as possible, and race back to the phone. But when I get back someone else is using the phone. "Come on, come on," I say under my breath.

The lady using the phone hangs up and gives me a dirty look. "It is a public phone, you know. Anyone can use it."

"I'm sorry," I say.

When she has gone I pick up the receiver, put in my money and dial the number of Dinnet Hotel to speak to Alice Macdonald.

The phone rings. And rings. And rings. She doesn't pick up and eventually it goes to answer-phone, but there's no point in leaving a message. She can't ring back.

I stand on Stramongate Bridge and watch the river in the rain. As it gushes over the weir it churns up the silt from the bottom. It's brown and murky, with white rollers. I've seen all sorts washed away in this river before now; branches, whole trees and even sheep. You can't stop it. You can't control it. You can't fear it. It does what it does and you just have to live with it.

I go back to the phone box, but the hotel answerphone is still on.

By the end of the afternoon I have probably walked miles, up and down the river watching the rain fall and the water rise. The Dinnet Hotel are not picking up any calls, I am cold and wet, and I feel both closer to Ziggy and further away at the same time.

Black Clouds
Papa Roach: Dave Buckner

When I get home, dinner is ready, and like, it's only four o'clock.

"Have you had a nice day?" says Dad. He's cheerful, and wearing the Led Zep t-shirt and Hawaiian shorts over his pyjamas again.

"Great thanks," I say. "But why are we having dinner now?"

Dad looks at the clock and sees the time. "I thought it was later," he says, shaking his head. "Oh well, never mind."

"Did you pick up Sam?" I check.

He nods and says, "Thank you for the note."

"In those?" I say, pointing at his pyjamas.

Dad looks down and shrugs. Well I suppose they could just about pass for casual wear.

We all sit down at the table. Dad has made macaroni cheese, chips and egg sandwiches. The sauce is a bit lumpy, the pan has a burnt brown sludge on the bottom, and the egg sandwiches are a weird touch, but Sam likes it because it's the yellowest meal he's ever had.

"So, have you had a nice day?" says Dad.

"You've already asked me that, but yes thanks," I say.

Sam giggles. "You asked me three times."

"Did I? Sorry," says Dad. "And what did you say?"

"I said it was a silly day and that we had to do outdoors PE in the rain, but Dan's mum came to pick him up with his new puppy and it has eaten one of Dan's slippers. You weren't listening."

"Yes, I remember now," says Dad.

When Sam has finished he takes his plate to the sink and asks if there is pudding. There isn't, so I give him the flying saucers from my bag and he goes off to play space aliens or something. This is a good time for me to show Dad Mr Badger's letter. I pull it from my school bag and put it on the table. I have butterflies in my tummy because I know I have a lot of explaining to do.

"What's this?" says Dad.

"It's a letter," I say. "From school."

"I can see that. I'm not stupid." Dad stands up and stacks the dishes for the washing up.

"Here, let me wash. You read," I say, nodding at the table.

Dad opens the envelope and pulls out the paper inside. I turn my back and wash the plates, rather than watch. The burnt cheese sauce needs soaking in the pan, but I wash everything else, all the while expecting some reaction, some comment from Dad.

When I have finished, Dad picks up a tea towel and start to dry plates. "So who have you been fighting?" he says.

"Dad, it was nothing. It was just Ebony and Alex Watson and it wasn't even really me. I was just protecting Dylan."

"Bob Dylan?"

I don't even know if that's supposed to be a joke, because Dad has a perfectly straight face. If it is, I don't laugh. "Dylan Bell," I say, exasperated.

146

Dad nods. "I know, I know." But does he?

He carries on drying up dishes and doesn't ask me any more questions. It doesn't feel as if he's really given the letter a lot of thought or that he's especially cross about it. And it's not that I'm some kind of weird masochist or anything but it's, like, frustrating not knowing what he thinks. So I say, "You will come won't you?"

"Come where?"

"To the meeting." I pick up the letter and wave it in front of Dad. "This meeting."

He takes the letter from me and reads it again. I watch his eyes darting along the lines, scanning the words. It seems to take him forever, and I swear he reads it about a dozen times. "And why do they need to see me?" he says, eventually.

"To discuss my attitude, and punctuality and stuff," I answer, kind of floored by his question.

"But shouldn't they be discussing that with you?"

I check to see if he's joking this time, but his face is totally straight. "Um, yes. But Mr Badger wants to talk to you as well," I say.

Dad pulls a face. "I don't really like meetings."

This is true. He doesn't really like people or leaving the house or anything. He used to. But he doesn't anymore. I try to imagine what Mr Badger and the Welfare Officer woman will say and think if Dad's not at the meeting. Is this how kids end up in care? Because Stacey Wilson was always at meetings before she got sent to a foster home.

"Dad, please, just come to the meeting," I say. "I don't want to go on my own."

"Of course I'll be there," he says.

It's all a bit surreal.

Of Wolf and Man
Metallica: Lars Ulrich

Sam has been unusually quiet all evening, playing in his room. At bedtime, I call up and ask if he would like a milky drink.

He comes down, clutching a piece of paper and shows it to me. "I started doing it in school and Miss Magick helped me, but I finished it all on my own," he says, dead proud.

It's got pictures all around the edge and writing in the middle. The pictures are of a big stick person and two small stick people; one of them is wearing a skirt and the other is carrying a kangaroo. The writing is one of those acrostic poems and it says:

*S*illy
*I*s kind
*S*umtims grumpy
*T*all
*E*nglesh
*R*eely good at drums
*F*unny
*A*llwaas kind
*T*eechar
*H*appy
*E*lvis
*R*oc Star
*M*onkey
*E*ars

"Aww, Sam. That's really really lovely," I say. "You are so clever. Except I am never grumpy." I pretend to be outraged and Sam giggles. "And what's this bit about Dad being a teacher."

"Dad said he was going to teach me how to play the guitar."

Because of the way Dad has been with his guitar lately, I doubt it will ever happen, but I try to be encouraging and say how lovely it would be.

"I'm going to show this to Dad," says Sam, disappearing into the living room, well-pleased with himself.

I go into the kitchen to make the milky drink, and because we ate so early, I make toast and jam too. I am just putting it all on a tray when I hear shouting from Dad and Sam.

I run into the living room to find Sam ripping up his poem, his eyes ablaze and his bottom jaw sticking out. Dad is obviously steaming, and his guitar is lying on the floor.

I pick up the guitar and say, "What happened?"

"He's not going to teach me guitar anymore," says Sam.

"I never said I would," says Dad.

"You did. Last week, you said it."

"No, Sam. I didn't."

"I don't think Sam would make it up," I say.

Dad thinks about this, then says, "Okay, well even if I did, I certainly wouldn't be teaching him on my Gibson, would I? You don't let piglets drive tractors!"

"What?" I haven't a clue what he's on about.

"I mean... I mean... Um... Oh leave me alone!" says Dad.

149

Sam's face crumples.

"What are you talking about piglets and tractors for?" I say.

"Just leave me!" shouts Dad.

I am properly shocked at Dad and I have no idea where he's coming from with this piglet/tractor thing.

Sam runs out of the room and stomps up the stairs. I want to stop and reason with Dad, but I know Sam's hurting so I follow him to his room where he is crying under his duvet.

"I hate Dad," he says.

I know he doesn't really hate Dad, but I'm not surprised he's upset. Dad's acting very weird. It's hard enough for me to understand and I'm nine years older than Sam. He lets me put my arm around him and he cuddles up to me. "Come on, let's choose a story," I say, because at least that feels as if it's the normal thing to do.

"Can we make one up? Take it in turns to do a line each," he says, which is a game we used to play when Sam was really small.

I agree on the condition that he brushes his teeth and puts on clean pyjamas, which he does in double quick time, before climbing back into bed with Martin. I close Sam's curtains, blocking out the stormy night and the almost full moon, then sit on his bed, take a couple of deep breaths to get in the right frame of mind for story telling, and begin.

"Once upon a time there was a boy called Sammy…"

"Who had an evil dad and a kind sister," he says.

"Okay. Well, the sister wasn't just kind, she was also really clever."

"And Sammy had special powers."

150

"Like?" I say.

"Like he could run really fast; faster than all the other kids."

"He sounds like a superhero," I say.

Sammy smiles. He'd love to be a superhero. "Yeah, except the evil dad doesn't know Sammy is a superhero."

"Why is he evil?" I say.

"Because," says Sam, "he's starting to grow hair on his chest, on the backs of his hands and his teeth are starting to grow long and pointy. And when the moon is full, he goes outside and howls… HOWWWLLLLL!"

I cover up my ears and pretend to be scared.

"He's an evil werewolf!" says Sammy.

I feel a bit uncomfortable about this. "I'm not sure the dad should be a werewolf," I say. I don't want Sam to have nightmares.

"It's only a story," he says. "Werewolves aren't real."

And I'm, like, "Well promise me that if you wake up in the middle of the night, dreaming about werewolves, you won't wake me up complaining."

"Dan told me all about werewolves," he says. "So I don't need to be scared."

"What did he tell you?"

"He told me they are just normal people who turn bad when it's a full moon."

I don't know if he's right or not. I've never been interested in paranormal stuff, but I'm sussed enough to work out that the characters in our made up story aren't a million miles away from me, Sam and Dad. "Why did you make Daddy be a werewolf?" I say.

"Because Daddy's changing into a horrible person," he says.

151

"I'm sure he didn't mean to be horrible to you," I say.

"I wrote him a poem about us and drew pictures and everything," says Sam.

"I know. And I'm sure he really liked that. But you know what?" I say. "I don't think Daddy's feeling very well and that can make you say and do funny things sometimes."

"What's the matter with him?" says Sam.

"I'm not really sure."

Sam looks worried. He hugs Martin real close and expects me to explain.

"I think he's got a headache or something," I say. "He'll be better tomorrow…" Even I can hear the doubt in my voice.

Sam nods. He's trying to be brave and not ask questions.

I reach for Mr Gum, trying to be brave too, and pretend everything is fine. "Here Sam, let's read this instead," I say.

I read the words, and Sam listens. Neither of us laugh. I get a hollow empty feeling in my stomach and I'm not sure if it's the lack of supper, or something else.

My Immortal
Evanescence: Josh Freese

Mum and I are on the way to school. I am about Sam's age. She runs ahead, stops and turns round with her arms wide open for me to run into. I run to her, and she picks me up and spins me round. We do it again and again, all the way to school. I am laughing and happy. When we get to the school gates, I don't want to let her go. I don't want to be on my own in the big scary school. When I turn around she's not there and I start to cry.

I wake up. My eyes are wet and my pillowcase is damp. I feel sick in my stomach and I am scared to close my eyes in case I dream again.

Running On Empty
Jackson Browne: Russ Kunkel

It is raining hard; proper grey-day-flat-sky rain like you only ever get in Cumbria.

After leaving Sam at Dale I cross over to use the phone box, but someone has puked in it and I can't stand the stench.

At Longpool, kids are coming out of the newsagent stuffing their faces with crisps and bars. It makes me feel hungry, and I realise I never had breakfast; which means Sammy never had breakfast either. And worse, I didn't do any lunches. What was I thinking? The thought of Sam's empty little belly while he watches all the other kids with their fancy packed lunches and school dinners makes me feel terrible. So I go into the newsagent and buy some pre-packed sandwiches, a packet of crisps and a carton of juice. I don't have enough money to buy anything else, but at least Sam will eat.

At the risk of being late, again, I turn around and head back to Dale.

I go straight to Sam's class and look through the steamed up glass. They haven't started the register and even though Sam sees me, he won't come over, so I knock and let myself in.

"Hello Daisy," says Miss Magick.

"I'm sorry to interrupt, but Sam forgot his lunch." I hold out the plastic bag with the pre-packed sandwiches and crisps.

Sam stays in his seat and gives me evil eyes.

"Sam?" says Miss Magick. "Your sister's brought your lunch."

"I've got lunch," he says, curling his lip.

"No you haven't," I say. "I got up late, remember?"

Curtis is sat next to Sam and he laughs. Sam's face goes red.

Rain water is dripping off my hair and I am cold. "Sam, just take this. You'll be hungry if you don't. Come on, or I'll be late."

Sam stays where he is, arms folded and determined.

Miss Magick comes over to me. "Shall I look after this?" she says. And as she does I have, like, this flashback of bread on the table and the knife sticking out of the butter, and an empty jar of jam and I realise Sam is telling the truth and I have just embarrassed him for nothing.

I feel stupid and self-conscious.

Miss Magick smiles and holds out her hand. "Are you all right?" she says. "You're very pale."

I give her the food and say, "I'm fine."

Except I'm not. Everything seems impossibly distant all of a sudden. The weight drains from my head and my heart beats faster and faster. I want to be outside, breathing air, but the room is starting to spin, my brain has gone swimming and my legs are made of jelly. I am falling...

Paranoid
Black Sabbath: Bill Ward

I wake up in the school office at Dale. I don't know how I got here. There is a cold flannel on my head and Mrs Grimes, the secretary, is next to me. She has some biscuits and a plastic cup of orange squash for me to drink. She says I fainted and they've tried to phone Dad but it's constantly engaged. I explain that it's broken.

"I'm going to drive you home when you feel better," says Mrs Grimes.

"I'm fine," I say. "I need to be in school." Mr Badger would probably have kittens if I was absent.

So Mrs Grimes phones Miss Canning and tells her what has happened and then says she will drive me to school instead.

In the car, Mrs Grimes asks me lots of questions about whether I am sleeping and eating properly and if I am trying to lose weight. I'm not. I wonder whether I should feel insulted, but decide I can't be bothered. I'll have enough to worry about once it gets around school that Mrs Grimes has driven me there.

I've missed first lesson, which was IT, and arrive in time for the start of Biology. Mr Mac is going to test our memory, and hands out question papers. It's a test about what we remember from the last lesson.

Question 1
Fill in the blanks in this sentence, using the word list below.

The ___ is the part of the brain responsible for ___ , ___ , ___ and ___ .

language - cerebral cortex - intelligence - memory - consciousness

Question 2
Memory is the ability to store and retrieve information. Short-term memory lasts for approximately how long?
- 30 seconds
- 30 minutes
- 30 hours
- 30 days
- The whole of your life

Question 3
Long-term memory may last for how long?
- 30 seconds
- 30 minutes
- 30 hours
- 30 days
- The whole of your life

Question 4
When your memory is full up, you have to get a new one. True or false?

Question 5
When you sing the words to your favourite childhood song, are you using your short term or long term memory?

Question 6
What is mild cognitive impairment?
- Chicken curry
- A subtle decline in memory and mental ability
- Low alcohol beer

Question 7
Dementia is from a family of illnesses to do with:
- Memory loss
- Bad fashion sense
- In-growing toe nails

Question 8
People with Alzheimer's disease suffer a loss of short-term memory. They may not remember what day of the week it is, but they can usually remember details of which of the following:
- Their childhood
- Their breakfast
- Their name

There are more questions, but I spend the rest of the lesson staring into space. Everyone else seems to find Mr Mac's memory test very funny. I just feel sick.

At break, I go to the library. I want to get on a computer and look up more about memory. There are places on the internet where you can type in symptoms and they give a diagnosis. Ebony and I used to mess about on them when we were in year eight, typing in a whole load of random symptoms and seeing what we came up with. It was funny then. It's serious now.

But the computers are all booked out. It's a wet break, so it figures. I hang around, watching kids play games when I've got serious stuff to do and eventually complain to a librarian. She tells me to come back later, but I wait anyway. No one moves, the bell goes, and I don't get a chance to look anything up.

After break it's maths.

I sail through with my eyes practically shut because it's all graphs and pie charts and it's easy. Mrs Pike keeps looking at me. She must know about the fainting and I know I have sags under the bags under my still red eyes, but she doesn't say anything.

At lunch, the computers are still booked up, so I go through to the dining hall, hoping to see Dylan.

Miss Canning's voice reverbs over the loud speaker announcing that the emergency services will be testing the flood siren in two minutes and it is just a practice so no one is to panic. It is noisy and steamy and smells of food. Kids are eating all sorts: paninis, baked potatoes and beans, salads, hot food and packed lunches. I try not to mind that I've spent all my money on Sam when I didn't need to.

I look around for Dylan because I want to apologise for the way I reacted yesterday, but I can't see him anywhere. I see Ebony and Emily and Sian and they see me too. They say something behind their hands, obviously about me and then fall about laughing. If only Dylan was here…

But suddenly the flood siren sounds…

WoooOOOoooOOOoooOOO…

…and the speakers are right above my head. It's deafening and hurts my ears. People jeer and whistle, making the noise so much greater than it should be. I turn to leave, but as I do, I trip over a bag and fall flat on my face.

"Stacked it!" shouts Alex Meat-head Watson, and all his cronies join in with a round of applause.

The contents of my bag spill out, and about five hundred kids are laughing at me. Totally mortified, I pick myself up, grab my stuff and get out of the dining hall as quick as I can. I wish I could leave, run away, be as far from school as possible. But there are teachers policing the doors because of the wet lunch and there is no way out. I am trapped.

My hands are rolled into fists and my arms are desperate to lash out.

If I don't break free of this day, somehow, I know I will do serious damage to something or someone and live to regret it.

There is only one escape…

Drumming Song
Florence and the Machine: Christopher Lloyd Hayden

In the music block, I sign myself in, grab some sticks and sit down at the kit. It's a Pearl; nothing fancy, just a bog standard bass, floor tom, rack, snare, ride crash and hi-hat. I take one deep breath and start hitting them, hard.

It's all about the anger and letting off steam. I bash the toms hard and want to break skins. Rage flies down my arms and I lash out, banging as loud and violent as I can. Then I crash on the ride and hi-hat and slam my foot hard on the bass pedal. Making a noise is my one and only goal, drowning out the future and the past, beating every beat in the present, the now, the moment.

And boy, how I've missed this feeling; just letting go, letting rip, letting something inside take over...

And then I hit the snare. You can't hit the snare without feeling your rhythm - right left right right - then after a while I add a double left into six eight time, picking up on the toms and bass. Right left right right kick kick – all around the kit... It's like fire - a tiny ember, a small flame and then whoosh! And before I even think about it I'm back in control and back on top.

I stay here, killing riff after roll, getting some crazy moves down and I swear, no one and nothing can touch me and for the first time in weeks, maybe months, I am me and I am free.

Bring Me Sunshine
Willie Nelson (acoustic)

I've been high all afternoon; ever since playing again.

Dylan didn't want an apology. He said he was just happy we were still friends. In music, Mr Strummer told him about me drumming and now we are walking and talking, with Loretta, about the band.

"Oh em gee, I can't believe it," squeals Loretta. "What shall we call ourselves?"

And Dylan is, like, the voice of sensibleness. "Let's get the music right first and think up a name afterwards."

And Loretta is, "Totally wiv ya, Dyl. What we gonna play?"

And we all fall about laughing, because we've got this mad bad band idea and everything, but we've never even played together before and we might really suck! I don't even care. After a terrible start it has turned out to be my best day in ages.

At home, Dad and Sam are watching TV. For once, I sit down and join them because it feels like the right thing to do. I'm happy. I'm going to be happy with my family. And Sam can see I'm in a good mood and maybe that rubs off on him a little because he lets me be in charge of the TV remote. Me + TV remote = unheard of!

I wait until the end of his programme, and then it's the adverts. The first one is an advert for Princess Sparkle, a doll with glittery hair and eyes which light up in the dark. The second advert is an ad for a remote control moon buggy. I flick between the channels trying to find something without adverts, but Sam grabs the remote back from me and says he wants to watch them.

"They're Christmas adverts," I say.

"So?" he says.

And Dad says, "Is it that time of year already?"

"Yeah," I say. "It gets earlier and earlier doesn't it?"

And Dad says, "Are Morecambe and Wise on this year?"

"Who?" says Sam.

"Morecambe and Wise. The funniest men alive," says Dad.

And I say, "I don't think either of them is still alive." I don't mean anything by it. It's just a throw away comment, but it's as if I have dropped a bomb in the room or something.

Dad says, "No! That's awful. What happened?" He looks genuinely upset too, as if this is the first time he's heard the news. But even when I was a kid and used to watch the DVD's with Dad and Ziggy, Morecambe and Wise weren't still alive. "I love Morecambe and Wise," he says. And then he starts singing. "Bring me sunshine, in your smile…" which is their theme tune, and Dad remembers every word.

I notice Sam staring at me, and register that my own face has frozen in this, kind of, horrified open mouthed mask. I cannot believe Dad would not know that Morecambe and Wise were dead.

Sam wants to know why I am so freaked out. He doesn't ask with words; he strokes my arm and looks up into my face, searching my eyes for an answer.

"Come on," I say, "Let's make some tea."

We go through to the kitchen, where I get out oven chips, sausages and peas. In the other room Dad's on his guitar playing the chords for Bring Me Sunshine. It's easy. He has no trouble with this song. I ask Sam to lay the table, which he does without any argument, while I lay out the chips and sausages on a baking tray.

Sam is quiet and I say, "Are you all right?"

He goes over to the misted up window and draws a sad face in the steam.

"Are you feeling sad?" I say, putting our food into the oven.

"No," he says. "Scared."

I put down the oven gloves and hold out my arms to him. He comes over and I hold onto him and stroke his hair. "What are you scared of, Big Boy?" I say.

Sam speaks quietly. "Of Daddy ..." He says it into my body and I can only just hear the words, but my heart misses a beat.

"I know," I say.

Sam looks at me. "Are you scared too?"

I nod.

He doesn't react and I don't know if I've made him feel better or worse.

Smile Like You Mean It
Killers: Ronnie Vannucci

I come downstairs to find Dad playing his guitar in the kitchen; the song he's been writing forever. He's still stuck. In fact he seems to have gone backwards with it.

Sam is awake and dressed for school. He has even made me some sandwiches and wrapped them in a little plastic bag with a post-it note on top. The post-it note says 'Daisy,' and has a sweet little flower drawing next to it.

"Awww, thanks Samster," I say and blow him a kiss.

Sam points a banana at me. "Kapow kapow!" he says, ducking behind a chair and knocking it over, before racing upstairs.

Dad laughs. He seems to be in a good mood.

"Did you actually go to bed?" I say.

"No," he says. "What's the point when I can't sleep?"

I grab a bowl and a spoon and pour myself some Frosties. Then I get the milk from the fridge, smelling it before I drown my cereal. It's fresh. I sit down next to Dad who is eating toast with jam.

"Dad," I say. It feels like I have nothing to lose. "I really think you need to see a doctor."

Dad puts down the toast and looks at me, straight. "I'm not taking sleeping pills if that's what you think."

I take a deep breath. "It's not about the sleeping. Well, not especially," I say. "It's more about, you know... generally. For a check up. Kind of." How do you tell someone you think they are ill without it sounding like you think they are ill?

Dad is looking at me. He's frowning.

"It's just … you know, the not sleeping, the getting muddled, the forgetting."

"I don't think a doctor can help me with that," he says. "It's just the way I am."

So I try and put it another way. "I just wondered if maybe you were a bit … depressed, a bit down. You know? Because you don't really go out anymore, and you seem to get upset about things, and like, all those things you forget..."

"It's hardly an illness," he says.

"No, but it happens so often." I say.

"It's who I am," says Dad. "Ask anyone."

"But it's not. Not really. In that letter from Ziggy…"

"What letter?"

"Dad," I say gently. "Ziggy wrote a letter to you and you showed it to me last week. Don't you remember?"

He doesn't answer.

"Ziggy said the band would never have got going without you. You wrote the music, you got them signed, you organised the tours."

Dad smiles, fondly. "I did, didn't I?"

I feel like I am on a roundabout. Maybe I'm wrong. Maybe I'm not. Maybe, I'm going crazy. But he just makes me feel so helpless.

Sam comes back in the kitchen wearing his school bag. I try not to let him see that I am upset. "We've got to go," he says.

"Is that the time?" I say, putting on my smiley face.

Dad sits back and folds his arms. He is staring at me. "Daisy?" he says.

But I don't want to have this conversation any more, not in front of Sam and there isn't time before school. I wish I'd never brought it up. It's just that Dad is staring at me and searching for some words and it's like a spell I can't break.

Dad grabs my hand and says, "I'm a selfish so and so, aren't I? You're worried and I should be listening to you…"

My eyes prickle. It isn't like Dad to admit someone else is right.

"… But you know how I feel about doctors."

Sam says, "Come on. I don't want to be late."

I pick up my sandwich and put it in my bag, then kiss Dad on the forehead. "We'll talk later, okay?" I say.

"Definitely," says Dad.

Do or Die
Papa Roach: Dave Buckner

After dropping Sam, I go straight to the telephone box on Gooseholme, hoping it has been cleaned. It has. The disinfectant smell is almost as bad as the puke, but I have to do this. Ziggy is, like, my one little ray of hope in all the dark stuff going on at home.

Alice Macdonald: "Alice Macdonald, Dinnet Hotel. Can I help you?"
Me: I don't know if you remember me. I'm Daisy Meadows, I rang before about…
Alice Macdonald: Ziggy! Och of course I remember you. We got cut off, didn't we?
Me: I ran out of money.
Alice Macdonald: I tried 1471 but I couldnae get through. I'm so so glad you rang back.
Me: Do you know where Ziggy is? You said he went travelling with Anna?
Alice Macdonald: I did. They wanted to get it out of their system before the baby came.
Me: The baby?!
Alice Macdonald: Aye, that's right. A wee boy. Called him Elvis, right enough.
Me: Elvis? When? What…? Where are they now?
(*I literally can't string a sentence together anymore*.)
Me: Because I'm, like, desperate to see him.
Alice Macdonald: Have you got a pen and paper? I'll give you the number…

"Daisy!" shouts Dylan, as I leave the telephone box. I turn to see him running towards me. "What were you doing in there?" he says, when he reaches me.

I am still in shock, but show him the phone number and say, "It's Ziggy's." My hands are, like literally, shaking.

"No way!" says Dylan. "How did you get that?"

I explain about Dinnet and going to the library and speaking to Alice MacDonald, and then I tell him how Ziggy apparently has a baby called Elvis.

"This is brilliant! Why don't you ring him now?"

"Now? … Well, I don't know if … if I'm ready?"

"Ready for what?"

"Ready to speak to Ziggy."

"Of course you are…" he says. Dylan doesn't seem to think it's a problem, ringing someone I haven't spoken to for years.

"But it's been a long time," I say. "And like, the reality of having this number is way different to the dream of wanting it. I need to pluck up some courage."

"Ziggy's your uncle! You don't need courage," he says.

If only life was that simple. "No. I think I'll leave it till later," I say. I'm not bottling it. I just want to make sure I say the right things.

I spend the day clock-watching and lurching between daydreams and daymares.

One minute I am thinking how Ziggy's going to make this big difference to Dad; as if just the shock of seeing Ziggy again will suddenly shake Dad out of his forgetfulness and start being normal again. And the next minute I'm thinking, Ziggy won't want to know. He hasn't been in touch for four years. He's got a new life now, with his own family. Why would he want to spoil that with our problems? The negative part of my brain seems to be stuffed with more questions than the positive side; not least of which is what if Ziggy doesn't want to speak to me?

In maths, Mrs Pike asks me if I am all right because I don't seem to be concentrating. In English, Mr Hardy suggests I would do more work sat outside the Head's Office. In Physics, Mrs Wilson blows a fuse and keeps me in for lunchtime detention.

I don't see Dylan all day, but at home-time he is waiting on the wall for me. "Do you want to use my phone?" he says.

And it's not that I'm not grateful, because I am, it's just that the argument in my head hasn't been resolved.

"What have you got to lose?" says Dylan,

"Maybe I should talk to Dad about this first?" I say.

"You can tell him afterwards," says Dylan. He takes his phone from his pocket and offers it to me. "Go on. You know you want to."

But I don't take it. "Not here," I say. "If I do ring Ziggy, I don't want it to be outside school with everyone listening."

Dylan understands this and we start walking down towards Gooseholme. I tell him my fears and he listens, but it's so obvious he still thinks I should ring Ziggy. Maybe I am more like Dad than I would care to let on, because the more Dylan tells me what to do, the more I feel myself resisting.

"Daisy, come on," says Dylan. "I'm getting frustrated with you now. This could change your life."

And like, because Dylan is my best friend and because he's always been there for me, I have to give in.

So I get out the number, take the phone and dial.

First the ringing.

Then the click. My heart is literally in my mouth.

I go over the words in my head, like, a whole speech in a split second.

I hear the voice...

"Ziggy Meadows is not available to take your call just now. Please leave a message after the fill."

There's a drum fill then; a six stroke roll of threes and sixes around the kit, which is probably wasted on most people. I just think, nice. And I'm, like, so concentrating on the fill that when the phone bleeps and I'm supposed to say something, I don't. I just stand there, with nothing in my head except an image of Ziggy playing drums.

So I hang up.

"He's not there," I say, to Dylan.

"Well leave a message," he says.

I try again.

First the ringing.

Then the click. And I go over the words in my head. Hi Ziggy, It's Daisy. Your niece. I really need to speak to you...

I hear the voice...

"Ziggy Meadows is not available to take your call just now. Please leave a message after the fill."

171

The six stroke.

The beep.

"Ziggy, it's Daisy…" My mouth is dry and the words have run away. I swallow and lick my lips with my tongue. "I need to see you," I say. "Um… Dad's not well… and I'm in trouble at school." My mouth dries up again because my eyes have got all the water. "I don't know what to do, and I don't even know where you are. We don't have a phone, so can you come? Can you come and see us? Like, today would be good…"

But suddenly, the impossibleness of everything just gets the better of me and I hang up.

"You did it!" says Dylan. "Well done."

He puts his arms around me, but I am filled with regret and the terrible feeling that I've done the wrong thing.

"He hasn't even bothered to contact us in four years. Why would he want to now?" I say, pushing Dylan's arm away.

"Daisy!" he says.

But I walk away. I should never have let him talk me into it. It was stupid stupid stupid and is probably going to make everything worse.

Before I Fall to Pieces
Razorlight: Andy Burrows

At home, Dad is still wearing his pyjamas, Led Zep t-shirt and Hawaiian shorts. Sam has a plastic bag tied around his waist with Martin sticking out. I'm guessing it's supposed to be a pouch.

They are playing a game called Celebrity Heads where they both have a picture of someone famous stuck on their forehead. They can't see their own picture, and they have to ask the other person questions to find out who it is. The other person can only answer yes or no. Dad has a picture of Cinderella stuck on his forehead and Sam has the Queen.

I go upstairs and change out of my wet clothes. When I get back down, Sam has correctly guessed the Queen, and Dad is asking questions about the Cinderella on his own head.

"What do I know already?" he asks Sam.

"She's a girl, she isn't a comedian and she isn't in a band," says Sam.

"Is she alive or dead?" says Dad.

"Yes or no questions only," Sam reminds him.

"Sorry. Is she dead?"

"No," says Sam, boinging up and down, and clapping excitedly.

"So she's alive," says Dad.

"No!" squeals Sam, delighted at being able to catch Dad out.

"Come on," says Dad. "She's either alive or dead. She's got to be one or the other."

I dare to suggest that the person Dad is guessing is not exactly a celebrity, and Sam is not happy with me. But it's not fair; Dad's struggling and he could do with some help.

"Who is it then?" he says.

"Guess," says Sam.

"How can I guess if I don't know whether she's alive or dead?"

"Because..." says Sam, tapping his nose.

"Because she's a character in a story," I say.

"Mr Gum?" says Dad.

Sam laughs. "He's a Mister. You're trying to find a Miss. My turn now..."

"I'll start dinner," I say, thinking I am better off leaving them to it.

In the kitchen, Dad has written a note to himself and stuck it on the fridge with a magnet. The note says:

ELVIS - TALK TO DAISY

It makes me smile because at least it means he remembered about talking to me. I wonder if he's ready for what I've got to say.

I open a can of soup and put a pizza into the oven.

I can hear Sam shouting and giggling over Celebrity Heads and it's good they're having fun, but I wish Dad would come and talk to me now. I make a mental list of the things I want to say, which starts with a reminder about tomorrow's meeting in school, continues with me insisting Dad sees a doctor, and ends with me telling Dad I've been in touch with Ziggy. I'm okay about the

174

first one, kind of; dreading the second and I really don't know how I feel about the last one. It could go either way.

I lay the table and when everything is ready, I go back to Dad and Sam for a quick round of celebrity heads.

But when I arrive in the living room, Dad and Sam are sitting, like literally, at opposite ends of the room with their arms folded, both sulking like six year olds.

"What's happening?" I say.

"Dad's a bad loser!" shouts Sam.

"Bambi is not a celebrity!" shouts Dad in response.

"At least you've heard of him!" shouts Sam.

On the floor are torn up pictures of Cinderella, The Queen, Bambi and guitarist Jimmy Page from Led Zeppelin. I pick the Jimmy Page picture up for a closer look. The picture has been torn from the Cosmopolitan article about band reunions. There's no way Sam would know a rock guitarist from the seventies.

"It's Jimmy Page," I say.

"I knew that," said Dad.

"But I didn't," says Sam. "How am I supposed to guess if I don't even know who it is?"

"Oh for Pete's sake," cries Dad. "Just get off my case!" And then he stands up, and walks out of the room.

"Dad!" I call, but he doesn't come back.

We hear the front door slam. I look out of the window and see him walking off into the rain in his pyjamas, Led Zep t-shirt and Hawaiian shorts.

Ready to Fall
Rise Against: Brandon Barnes

I am staring out of the window into the rainy dark night, wishing I could turn back the clock. But how far would I go? A day? A week? A month? A year? Six years? I don't know when things started going bad.

Sam was in bed for an hour. He didn't want to go in the first place, but now he's back, standing in the doorway, holding Martin and crying. When I look at him, he runs and buries his head in my tummy and I wrap my arms around him. We sit in the dark together. I daren't speak for ages because I am afraid of what will come out.

After a while, Sam sniffs and pulls away. "Is Daddy still out there in his pyjamas?"

I nod. "Are you worried?" I say, trying to sound calm and in control.

Sam sniffs. "Yes."

"Me too," I say. "A little bit."

Sam looks out of the window and back at me.

"Where do you think he is?" he says.

"I don't know." I am scared Dad will never come back. I feel so helpless just sitting here, and I want to go and look for him. But I can't leave Sam.

Eventually, brave Sam says it. "Let's go out and look for Daddy. Just in case he's lost himself."

Sea of Madness
Iron Maiden: Nicko McBrain

The wind is picking up and the rain is gusting almost horizontally. Black clouds race across the sky and every now and again they break up, just long enough to see the full moon.

"Where do you think he is?" he says.

"I don't know. Where would you go if you were feeling upset?"

"The park," he says. "To play on the swings. What about you?"

"The castle," I say.

Holding hands, we go straight down the hill to Abbot Hall Park play area. Sam is shivering despite the jumper, the fleecy and the waterproof I made him wear. There's no sign of Dad or anyone else, and I didn't honestly think there would be, but at least we're doing something.

On Waterside, the river has begun to lap over onto the path. When we get on the footbridge, it shakes in the wind and Sammy doesn't like it, so I keep hold of his hand and try not to look down. On the other side of the river, houses on Aynam Road have sandbags in front of their doors.

Sammy stops. He looks up the hill at the Castle and says, "I don't want to go up there. It's really really dark."

I'm not sure I do either, so we decide to walk up Aynam Road instead, onto Gooseholme and then double back through town. The wind and rain beat straight into our faces and we have to lean forward at, like, forty-five degrees just to keep upright. All I can think about is finding Dad.

At Gooseholme, the river is on the footpath. I've never seen it this high before. There are some late night sightseers out watching, and for a minute or more I am fixated too; on the volume and power of so much water pushing past.

But Sammy says, "I'm scared." His skinny little body is shivering uncontrollably and his lips look almost blue. I don't feel brave anymore, just stupid for coming out in this. Dad's probably home by now, in the warm and dry, thinking we're upstairs in bed.

The padlock on the pitch and putt hut is broken and the door is banging about in the wind. "Let's shelter in there." At least it will be out of the rain.

We go inside. The door won't stay shut, so we hide behind the counter out of the wind. Above us are the shelves with putters and golf balls, course markers and an old green gardener's type jacket. I drape the jacket over Sam for extra warmth and we huddle together. Rain drums on the roof and on the metal window shutters and the door bangs open and shut. Sam is shaking with cold and fear, so I sing a song to occupy his mind; one of Dad's.

"I'm getting out of this place, I'm gonna have it all
Gonna dance on the moon, you gotta give me a call
I can't do it alone, I want you by my side
Baby baby baby take a rocket ride, with me… "

And Sam joins in. He used to love that song when he was little kid because of the line about the rocket ride.

And for a while, we sing at the tops of our voices. But the storm gets louder, the shutters rattle harder and the wind whistles sharper and we can hardly hear ourselves. This is the loudest storm I have ever heard. And then, something even louder rips across the wind.

WoooOOOoooOOOoooOOO…

No Prayer for the Dying
Iron Maiden: Nicko McBrain

Sam screams and blocks his ears with his hands. I wrap my arms around him. "It's okay Sam; it's okay. It's just the flood warning."

"But there's going to be a flood!" he cries.

"It's only a warning. It just means we should probably get out of here." I hold his hand and Sam squeezes tight, almost as if he's afraid I will just slip away.

Outside the hut, we get knocked back by wind and driving rain. The sightseers have disappeared, the river is washing onto the grass and the path has completely disappeared under water. I remember Dad's TV programme about bridges getting swept away by the force of the water and realise with horror that we'll need to cross a bridge if we want to go home.

"Are we going to drown?" says Sam. "Can we go back to our house?"

I want to, but I daren't risk it. "We'll go up to the castle," I say. "We can shelter in the ruins; at least we'll be safe."

Sam's not happy, but he doesn't get a choice. I take him down the cycle path and through Fletcher Park. The conker trees are creaking and waving about wildly. Sam thinks they are going to fall over and crush us. I promise him they won't, but what do I know? We go through the kissing gate and up the hill, with mud splashing our legs and our clothes are totally saturated. Even I am beginning to feel cold now.

Before we reach the cemetery Sam says, "I'm not going near the graves, not in the dark."

A break in the clouds reveals the moon, glowing white and fully round.

Sam stops, shakes his arm free of my hand and says, "There might be werewolves. Look at the moon. I want to go home."

"Come on, Sam," I plead. "We don't want to stay out in the rain all night, do we?"

But Sam won't move. "There might be werewolves in the castle too. Suppose they don't like the rain either and they're all there having a picnic?"

"There's no such thing as werewolves," I say. "You said so yourself."

"But what if there is?" he says, crying now. "And they've got hairy hands and pointy teeth and they come out and bite you and... and…"

He's tired and I'm tired. I don't have the energy to argue anymore and start walking on up, towards the castle ruins and shelter, thinking Sam will follow. But when I turn back to check, he's sitting down in the mud and the wind and the rain, and above all the noise of the storm he is screaming, "I want Daddy!"

I am going nowhere.

The wet on my own face turns to tears.

My choices have all run out.

I walk back down the hill and sit in the mud next to Sam.

Great Gig in the Sky
Pink Floyd: Nick Mason

I've failed. I've failed at school, I've failed to find Dad and I've failed at looking after Sam. I've failed at life.

If Dad really does have a forgetting disease, I've just proved without any doubt that we need to be taken away and looked after by someone who knows how to do it properly, just like what happened to Stacey Wilson.

Sammy and I sit in silence.

Above us, the clouds are beginning to clear and the moon is shining through. I am beginning to see the stars.

Below us, the cemetery makes me think about Mum and about dying. I think a lot about death. What happens when you die? Do you know you're dying? Does your heart stop working before your brain or do you keep on thinking for a bit after the last heart beat? And what about all the things you know, the things you've learnt in life and the feelings you've felt and the memories you've made? Where do they go? Is death really the end of everything or do you live on?

And what about Dad? What if Dad dies too?

I don't have any answers, but this much I do know: whatever happens next, when we do find Dad, I am going to make the most of the time we have left as a family.

Nothing Else Matters
Metallica: Lars Ulrich

It is almost dawn when we arrive home. Dad's wet clothes are lying in a heap on the kitchen floor, and he is fast asleep in his bed. We change into our pyjamas and I make Sam some hot milk and a hot water bottle, then tuck him into bed with Martin.

"That was quite an adventure, Samster," I say. "You're the bravest boy I know." He's not too tired to smile.

I want to wake Dad and talk, to tell him about Ziggy and how Ziggy has called his baby Elvis. I want to remind him about the meeting, and I want to tell him about how Sam and me went to look for him and got stuck in a storm instead... But I don't, because just now, it feels right to be on my own.

I put the washing into the machine, make myself a hot cup of tea with two sugars and open the front door to make friends with the now still night. The wind and rain have stopped and there is a feeling of peace in the air. The moon is already on the way, and over in the east I can see an orangey yellow glow of morning sun.

I've like, totally messed up this term, but I can't change the past and there's no point in worrying about the future because it hasn't happened yet. This moment is the only moment there is to make things right. This moment is all there will ever be. And in this moment everything is possible.

This isn't Giving Up. This is Letting Go
Rise Against: Brandon Barnes

I'm ready for school, but Dad and Sam are both fast asleep. I am not going to wake them. Sam will be too tired to go to school anyway, and after everything that's happened I would rather face Mr Badger on my own.

Being honest about my fears for Dad and our future may be easier if he's not there. And if it's not, then I'll live with the consequences.

But before that, there is still something I need to sort out. I need to see Dylan. Whatever has happened and will happen between us, I don't want to lose his friendship.

I go straight to his house and Elaine answers the door.

"Daisy!" she looks properly shocked to see me. "Are you okay? You look as if you've been up all night?"

She shows me into the kitchen, where Dylan is eating breakfast. "Oh Daisy, you look awful. Do you want some toast?" He comes over to me and puts his arms around me. I don't want to push him away ever again.

"I've come to say sorry," I say.

"What for?"

"For being an arse."

Dylan laughs. "You are no such thing."

"I was mean to you the other day. I still want to be friends."

Dylan says, "I was hoping we were more than that." He steps back and puts his hand under my chin, lifting my face gently till our eyes meet. "But I know you have stuff to deal with, so there's no hurry. Just know that I'm here for you."

I hold Dylan's hand and look into his deep brown eyes. Moments like this should be treasured and I don't want to move away, but outside I can hear Elaine revving up the camper van and I know we have to go to school. We pull apart.

But there's one more thing I need to ask. "I don't suppose Ziggy rang back did he?" I know the answer because Dylan would have told me, but I still need to hear it.

"Sorry," says Dylan.

We leave the house, together. The rain has completely stopped and there is blue sky beyond the clouds and the raindrops and puddles reflect the sunshine.

Despite everything, I feel all right.

Simple Truth
Power of Now: Ziggy Meadows

When we get to school Mr Badger is on yard duty and comes charging towards us. Dylan kisses my cheek and puts his arms round me. I smell his honeyed hair and feel the warm protection of his body.

"Daisy. Your father?" he says, looking behind me, expectantly.

"No, Mr Badger."

"But the meeting? It's an important meeting. I need your father to be here."

"I'd rather see you on my own," I say.

"But… but…" He looks behind me again and sees that he is powerless to change anything. He frowns and says, "Okay, well you'd better come inside anyway. We'll decide what to do about your father later."

Dylan squeezes my arm before I follow Mr Badger into the building. As I go through the door I turn to see him blowing me kisses.

Mr Badger tells me to wait outside his office while he makes some calls and I sit on the grey chairs. People are still arriving in school and there is a lot of busyness, especially at reception. A woman I don't recognise, wearing a smart suit is shown into Mr Badger's office and then Mrs Pike arrives. After the start-of-school-bell rings, Miss Canning tells me to go in. The chairs are arranged in a circle and there are two empty seats next to Mrs Pike. She gestures for me to sit on the one beside her.

My tummy starts churning, and despite the urge to run away, I sit down

Mr Badger introduces the woman in the suit; Miss Kelly the Educational Welfare Officer. He tells me she is here to help and says that she may have some questions; all I have to do is be straight and honest.

"I've got something I'd like to say first," I say. I am literally shaking. I am holding my own hands to keep them still but it's not working. "About my dad."

Mr Badger tips his head to one side. He nods, and I take this as my cue to speak.

"My dad isn't here because he's in bed. I didn't wake him because we had a bit of a weird night last night..." I explain about Dad walking out on us in his pyjamas and shorts and t-shirt, and how we went to look for him in the rain. My eyes start to water and I wish they wouldn't, but I can't seem to stop it happening. Mrs Pike hands me the box of tissues from Mr Badger's desk. I take one and continue. "But the thing is, like, it's not just last night. Dad's behaviour, and especially his memory, seems to be getting worse."

There's a long silence. Everyone is waiting for me to explain; even me. I have the words in my head but it's as if saying them will make everything real.

Mrs Pike speaks first. "You're worried about your dad's behaviour and his memory?" she says.

"I... I think he might have a forgetting disease because we did about it in Biology and... and I tried to find out more about it, but I never got the chance..."

And something kicks in then, something I can't explain; it's just that suddenly the words flow. I tell everyone about Dad's forgetfulness and his clumsiness, his lack of patience, his choice of outfits and how he can remember stories from his childhood but can't remember what day of the week it is. I tell them about how embarrassed I've been and how I stopped people coming to my house and I've been bullied; how I am scared of them taking me and Sam into care if Dad really is ill. I tell them that I never even showed Dad the first letter home because I didn't want him to worry and that even when I showed him the second letter he didn't seem to understand what this was all about.

And they listen. No one interrupts. I talk myself out, literally, like, till I've got nothing else to say.

And when I have finished, Mr Badger breaks the silence. "I'm so sorry for you." He seems really moved and even upset, and for the first time since I've known him, he too is lost for words.

Miss Kelly says, "I don't think there's any question of taking you, or your little brother, into care. We'll need to speak to your father, but we don't break up families lightly, whatever you may have been led to believe."

Relief floods into every bone, every muscle and every cell of my body and for the briefest moment it feels like floating. Mrs Pike says the meeting is over for the time being. They would like to talk to my dad and work out how best to help me. Miss Kelly says there are things which can be put into place to help me and Sam and that she will liaise with Mr Badger and meet me one day next week. She mentions the young carers support group and something about extra curricular support, but it's all a bit over my head. Nothing is how I expected it to be.

Mrs Pike wonders if I would like to go home after having such a disturbed night. Mr Badger thinks it's a good idea and I agree. Mrs Pike says she will drive me there.

Rock n Roll
Led Zeppelin: John Bonham

While I wait in the front entrance for Mrs Pike to get her keys, my eyes fix on a large silver van pulling into the car park. I recognise the faces inside immediately, but I can hardly believe what I'm seeing. And it's all happening in slow motion, like, nothing else is real.

The van parks...

The driver and passenger speak to each other...

The driver gets out and walks around to open the passenger door ...

The driver holds out his hand and helps the passenger down from the high seat...

Their faces are identical, although one looks considerably older than the other. And the older face, the one ravaged by rock and roll calls my name. "Daiiiiisyyyyy!" he cries, roaring across the car park as if I'm deaf. "What's the difference between a Dominos pizza and a drummer?"

I know the answer. The pizza can feed a family of four. And considering the circumstances, I shouldn't be laughing, but I am because it's Ziggy.

I run over to him and fling my arms around him. He lifts me up and swings me around, and then he repeats my name, over and over again. When he finally puts me down, I look at Dad. He is smiling and looks almost normal except that he is still wearing his slippers.

"Where's Sam?" I say. "I left him in bed. We had a bit of a disturbed night..."

Ziggy says, "Sam's safe. He's at home with his Auntie Anna and little cousin…"

"Elvis!" I say.

"Yeah, my little boy!" He stands back then and looks at me. He's serious. "I hope I'm a better dad than I have been an uncle. And I am so so sorry we lost touch. When I got your call, it was … well, it was amazing to hear your voice. I picked it up last night but it was late, and what with the weather and everything… I came as soon as I could."

My eyes are full of water. I don't know why. And I can see that Ziggy has also welled up. We hug one more time, and Dad joins in. This is how we used to be, before Mum died, before Sam was born, before all the bad stuff started. The three greatest rock musicians who ever lived.

October Playlist

Awake and Alive
Skillet: Jen Ledger

After school, Elaine picks us up in her camper van - me, Dylan and Loretta – The Band! We drive to my house where Sam and Dad are waiting with Ziggy, and we load up my drum kit. Elaine says I can keep my kit in Cath's spare room indefinitely.

A week after Ziggy returned we finally persuaded Dad to go the doctors. Dad didn't want to go but everyone sort of, well, ganged up on him. He admitted he was scared, but Ziggy said that was the best reason to go.

"What if there's nothing wrong?" Ziggy said. "You need to know."

And Dad was like, "But what if there is?"

And Ziggy was, "You still need to know."

You can't argue with that.

The Doctor spent a long time talking to Dad and Ziggy about how things are in Dad's life. He tested his eyes and his hearing and took some blood samples and stuff, and he got Dad to fill in this TYM sheet. (TYM = Test Your Memory.) Dad had to write down his name and date of birth and how old he is, and then answer questions, like, who is the Prime Minister? Why is a carrot like a potato? List four creatures beginning with the letter S, answer some simple sums, and he had to read a sentence which he had to remember at the end of the test. Ziggy said Dad just couldn't keep it in his head.

193

The Doctor said he would refer Dad to a Neurologist who's going to do a brain scan and rule out other conditions, like brain tumours and stuff. Nothing's definite. We have to wait and see how things develop.

While Dylan and Loretta lug everything upstairs, Elaine asks me if I am okay. She knows a lot about Alzheimer's and dementia because of where she works. I don't know why, but when I talk to Elaine it makes me want to cry. Maybe it's because she understands about memory diseases or maybe it's because she's Dylan's Mum and I've known her forever, or maybe it's just because Elaine is so nice. I feel better being here. Safer. Like, Elaine's been through awful times too and she's come out the other side. Being with Elaine makes me feel as if I can survive too.

Dylan comes into the kitchen carrying his guitar. He sees my red eyes and comes over to hug me. Elaine leaves us alone.

"Are you okay?" he says.

"I'm fine. It's just Elaine being supportive and lovely, kind of set me off. Know what I mean?"

Dylan smiles and strokes my cheek with his finger.

"We don't have to do this today," he says.

"No, I want to," I say, and when I think about it, add, "I need to actually. This is really important to me."

I take the crumpled piece of paper from my pocket and spread it out on the table. They are the lyrics to the song Dad is writing. After Ziggy told me about Dad's almost-diagnosis, I realised it would never get finished. Ziggy and I talked about it and he suggested I take it away and work on it myself. Dad has agreed to me doing this. His verse remains the same…

Half a lifetime torn away
And I'm breaking more with every day
I've had good times, and bad times
And I wish I had the key,
To turn back time and find that piece of me…

I've added some more verses and a chorus to finish the song and I've worked out the tune and chords on the keyboard. Dylan and Loretta are going to write the band music with me and we are planning to play the song at the Battle of the Bands. I watch Dylan reading, waiting for his reaction. Sharing this song makes me nervous because it's so personal. It started out as a song about Mum and now it's a song about Dad.

When he finishes reading, he stands there for a moment, then puts the paper down and says, "Daisy, it's beautiful."

Relief washes over me and I, like literally, breathe again. It's as if I've passed my GCSE song writing or something!

Upstairs in Cath's spare room, I play Dylan the tune then Dylan and Loretta work out chords and bass lines. I pick up some sticks and can't stop myself from playing along. It's just soooooo nice to be making music again. I feel alive and I never want this feeling to go away.

This Is Not An Exit
Seafood: Caroline Banks

Ziggy and Anna have taken Sam and baby Elvis to see their new house. It's the four-bedroom semi Dylan's Mum and Geoff went to view, and rejected. As soon as Ziggy saw it he was, like, "It's perfect for us. We'll be nearby to help Daisy and Sam and look after Elvis." And Anna was really delighted because it has a great big garden for little Elvis and beautiful views over the fells, to remind her of her Scottish roots.

While they are gone, I help Dad turn out his cupboards and his drawers. He has all sorts of memorabilia and clothes from years and years ago; stuff he'll never use again and he wants to be organised while he still remembers what everything is. Dad has little or no recollection of some of the more recent things he has hidden away, but some of the older stuff goes back to when he was a teenager and it's full of memories.

He pulls a pair of trousers from a box under his bed and gasps. "Well I never!" They have really really wide flares and a stars and stripes pattern. They are amazing!

"These were my Lucky Loons," he says.

"Why do you call them that?"

"Loons, because that was the style – don't ask me why because I don't know. Lucky, because I wore them the day I met Mum," he says

I sit next to him on the bed. "They are really weird," I say, looking at huge flares.

And Dad laughs. "I got the leg stuck in her front door!"

"You didn't," I say, laughing too.

"I'd just walked her home and we'd said goodnight and she went in the house and shut the door. When I turned to walk away, I fell over! The flare was stuck."

"Were you all right?"

"Yes, except I couldn't get my trousers free without knocking on the door and waking up the house, and I didn't want to do that in case Mum got in trouble for being late home…"

"And?"

"And so I took them off and went home in my underpants!"

I have an image of Mum opening her front door in the morning to find Dad's trousers on the step and it cracks me up. Tears of laughter roll down our cheeks.

This is the Dad I know and love.

Ziggy, Sam and little Elvis arrive home. Sam is very excited to tell us that Elvis can say his name and how he held his hand while they walked around the new house together. It's like, Sammy + Elvis Jnr = best mates.

We eat our tea in front of the TV. The toy adverts are getting closer together and Anna says, "Christmas is getting earlier every year."

Dad says, "Are Morecambe and Wise on? I love Morecambe and Wise."

"Not this year," says Ziggy.

"The funniest men alive," says Dad.

Sam looks at me and raises his eyebrows and I just say, "We could watch them on DVD if you like."

When Ziggy and Anna have to go home, I am sad. Sam doesn't want them to go either and hangs onto Ziggy's arm, saying, "Please stay. I'll let Elvis play with Martin." Like, that's the biggest gift he could think to give anyone.

"I'm coming back very soon, Kid," he says. "Got a house to paint and a couple of my favourite people I need to check up on."

"Favourite people?" says Sam.

"Us," I say.

Ziggy turns to me. "I will ring you every night, and every morning too if you want." He's bought and installed a new house phone for us and set me up with a new mobile. "We're doing everything we can to hurry this house sale through, but I want you to know I'm always here for you."

We do family hugs - Anna and little Elvis and Dad and Sam and Ziggy and me - but we can't hug forever. We have to say goodbye.

As they drive away, Dad says, "I'm still the good looking one." He has a twinkle in his eye when he says it.

Beneath The Blue Sky
Go-Gos: Gina Schock

It's the night before the competition.

Ziggy is staying with us to finalise the house sale and to watch the Battle of the Bands and I'm going over to Dylan's to practise. Before I leave, Dad gives me a kind of pep-talk. He tells me how the night before a gig things usually go wrong. "But it's nothing to worry about. It's as if you have to clear all the problems out of the way. All I'm saying is, whatever happens tonight, don't let it put you off balance."

I'm grateful for the advice, and hate the thought of his years of experience not being there forever. I really want him to come and see me play in a band before it's too late, and I know it's a lot to ask, what with Dad hating loud noises and everything, but I ask anyway. "Are you coming to watch us?"

He hesitates. Ziggy puts his hand on Dad's shoulder, as if he's urging Dad to say yes. And Dad says, "Try and stop me, Daisy."

And that makes me feel happy and unbelievably excited.

Only a Heartbeat Away
Vixen: Roxy Petrucci

Dylan and Loretta and I practise over and over again. Dad was right; we all mess up and at first it feels like more things go wrong than go right. But we don't lose our heads and gradually, bar by bar we get the song sounding as good as it can be.

We have to stop playing at nine because of the neighbours. Loretta has to go home soon after. It's just me and Dylan left. We sit on the floor in Cath's spare room, our music room, surrounded by wires, amps, drum bits and empty coke cans and talk about tomorrow.

"Watson's got a band together you know," says Dylan.

I did know, but I'm trying not to think about Watson.

"They're playing Smells Like Teen Spirit."

It's a classic, and if they do it well everyone will love it. We're playing a song nobody has ever heard. "We're going to have to be brilliant to ace that," I say.

"We are brilliant though," says Dylan, his sunshine smile as bright as ever.

"Yey!" I say, turning to face Dylan. "Big up for the…"

And before I can finish the sentence, he is leaning forward and our lips touch; softly, gently. Every nerve ending in my body bursts into bliss and behind my closed eyes, it's as if colours explode in my head.

Dylan's lips press against mine, and his hand caresses the side of my face. We move our mouths, kissing, tiny gentle kisses, feeling every moment as if it was the only moment. Everything before this and everything after this is just distraction. The kiss is the only thing that matters.

Romance
Wild Flag: Janet Weiss

Rudy is the first person I see when I arrive in the school hall. He's with a team from Kendal College setting up the lights and sound and recording equipment.

"I didn't know you'd be here," I say.

"It's part of our course," he says. He looks at the clipboard in his hand and runs his fingers down the order sheet. "You're on last," he says. "Is that okay?"

I'm not sure my nerves will hold out but it's not as if I have a choice. "Yeah," I say.

"What are you playing? I've never heard of it," he says.

"Something we wrote ourselves," I say.

I see a flash of surprise on Rudy's face.

"I know it's risky, but it's important to us," I say. "And my dad and my uncle and my little brother are coming to watch."

"Power of Now? They're coming here?" And he's so excited, like, as if my family are big celebrities. I think about how Watson's been calling Dad a washed up has-been for so long now, I'd forgotten that he's actually done something pretty remarkable. And that makes me feel good.

Out of the corner of my eye I see Loretta arrive. I call her over and introduce her to Rudy.

"Oh em gee," she says. "Look at all this techy stuff. Do you actually know what to do with it? I mean, you must be so clever. Is it difficult? Because I would love

202

to know what's what and how it fits together..." She's off on one of her can't-get-a-word-in-edgeways rants, but I can see that Rudy is totally captivated by her. Well, who wouldn't be?

I leave them alone and watch the other bands arrive for the warm up.

New Beginning
Girlschool: Denise Dufort

The hall lights go down and the coloured lights go up. The place is full, both with kids and teachers and there's a lot of cheering, clapping and whistling. Loretta is *helping* Rudy on the sound desk. Dylan and I are sat at the back. I am half watching the door, waiting for Dad and Sam and Ziggy, and half watching the stage.

Mr Mac announces the first band. They are called Lego Soldiers. They are year eights and play American Idiot. It's fun, it's bouncy and the singer is way out of tune but it doesn't matter. Everyone is dancing and whooping and being totally supportive. It's a great start. Dad, Sam and Ziggy arrive half way through. Sam rushes over to Dylan and hangs onto his arm. Dad and Ziggy stand next to me. When Lego Soldiers finish, they get great feedback from the crowd. Ziggy is well impressed, but Dad looks uncomfortable.

"Are you all right?" I say.

He nods, but I can tell he hates it.

The next band up are Princess; a year nine girl band who play Killer Queen. They've got some nice harmonies in there and I like them. I didn't know we had another decent girl drummer in the school and it makes me happy. Ziggy likes it too, but Dad looks grey. I am not sure he's going to make it through the night.

The next band is a guitar duet. Dominic and Leanne. Year 12's. They slow the tempo with the Bob Dylan classic, Make You Feel My Love. They are really really good. Dad enjoys it too; he can cope with the noise level and he's impressed by the guitar playing.

Dylan holds my hand and whispers, "Wow!" into my ear. So far, Dominic and Leanne are the toughest competition. The audience obviously love them too because they get massive applause and plenty of whooping.

Loretta comes to stand with us for the next song. "Oh em gee they were soooo cool," she says. "I'm literally petrifiable now."

"Have you all got collywobbles?" says Sam.

"Yeah, something like that," I say.

"But you're still going to win aren't you?" he says. I wish I shared his belief.

Mr Mac introduces Iron Gaga, the next band on stage. They are year elevens and play a kind of heavy metal version of Bad Romance; an Iron Maiden/Lady Gaga fusion. It's a good idea but the drums are all over the place, the guitars are just loud and screeching and the singer is more death growl than Gaga.

It's all too much for Dad and he walks away. Sammy runs after him and Ziggy looks at me and mimes over the noise, "What should I do?"

"Go after them," I mime back. As much as I want Dad and Ziggy and Sam to be here for me, I know it's more than Dad can stand. Even some of the kids in the audience have put their fingers in their ears.

Dylan stands behind me and puts his arms around my shoulders. He knows how important it is to have Dad at my first band gig, and he knows what it means to see Dad walk away. Loretta too. She puts her arm through mine. United we stand; one of us about to fall to pieces and the other two doing their very best to hold me together. I do my best not to cry.

When Iron Gaga finish, Mr Mac goes on stage. "A spectacular display of risk taking on all counts; let's hear it for our brave Year Elevens!"

There is some applause and some whistling, and the boys in the band look pretty pleased with themselves. I guess if they've had a good time, that's the important thing.

"Our penultimate band," says Mr Mac, "Are The Best Band What Ever Lived. No, seriously, that's their name, and it's up to you decide if it's true. Please give a big hand to TBBWEL and Smells like Teen Spirit."

Watson has all his cronies and meat-head friends in the hall and they push their way to the front. I see Ebony there with Emily and Sian. As soon as the band strikes their first chord, Watson's mates all start moshing and falling into each other. The techies turn on the dry ice and the lights go right down. For a minute or two it's crazy and funny and dark. Watson doesn't do a bad job at the back and the singer, Tom Martindale, is really good. But then the lights go up and Mr Mac and the teachers rush in and pull everyone apart, then stand at the front policing the crowd. It's a shame; as much as I'd like to beat Watson, The Best Band What Ever Lived are actually quite good and the crowd loves them.

Momentarily, it distracts me from my nerves.

But as soon as it's over, my stomach is, literally, churning over and over. I look around the hall to see if Ziggy and Sam and Dad have returned. But I can't see them anywhere. I don't want to play anymore and stand still at the back of the hall.

"Come on," says Dylan.

"I can't," I say.

Dylan grabs my hand and looks me at me straight. "We need to go on, now. Play it like he's watching anyway…" He squeezes my hand and I follow him to the stage.

It takes a minute to mic me up. I'm the first drummer to sing and they need to get the sound levels right. Loretta's on bass and Dylan is playing guitar.

I count us in with my sticks, 1, 2, 3, 4… And we're off…

"Half a lifetime torn away
And I'm breaking more with every day
I've had good times, and bad times
And I wish I had the key
To turn back time and find that piece of me…"

We get it better than it's ever been. It's almost perfect. Dad was right – the last run through got rid of all the problems and it's true to say we peak just when we need to.

When we reach the end, the kids in the hall cheer and scream and clap. I have goosepimples all down my body and I put so much of myself into playing, I can't move. I am exhausted. But happy. It's the single best thing I have EVER done in my entire life, and I know that I never want it to end. I want to play in a band forever. I need to play in a band forever.

Drumming is my heartbeat.

When the applause stops, Mr Mac thanks us and announces a refreshment break while the judges decide on the winner. As we leave the stage I look into the hall, hoping to see Dad.

But he's not there.

Everyone is stopping us and telling us how amazing we were and how they loved the song and I'm pleased. I get a buzz out of this, but there's a piece of me missing; the piece that's family. If only Dad had been here. I think about the years I have ahead of me, playing drums, being in a band and I wonder if he'll ever be there.

There is a tap on my shoulder. Not a nasty tap, but a gentle tap. I turn round and it's Ebony. "Fair play," she says. "You were really excellent."

I didn't expect that.

Loretta and Rudy are hitting it off in the corner, and me and Dylan are in the middle of drinks and crisps when Mr Mac announces the adjudication. All the band members need to go up to the stage. Dylan grabs my hand and Loretta comes over and grabs the other. We stand back, behind Iron Gaga and Princess who jostle to be nearest the front.

Mr Mac does his spiel about there being an awful lot of talent in the school and how proud he is to be part of an institution which supports and encourages young people to do what they love doing most. He gets a lot of whistles and cheers for that. Then he introduces the judges; the local mayor, a local businessman and Mr Strummer, the music teacher.

In third place, it's Dominic and Leanne. They get a massive applause. I'm thinking, if they've only come third, we can't possibly win.

In second place, The Best Band What Ever Lived. They too get a massive applause and whistling and foot stamping and the crowd at the front start moshing.

But in first place, "And I don't think there ever was any question about this. Not only did they perform beautifully, but they wrote the song themselves... it's Simple Truths, singing All There Is."

It's like a fairytale. Everyone loves us. They chant our name and whistle and clap and stamp their feet louder than I've heard all night. From failing at life to being a total winner in almost every sense of the word in half a term. We are all on a high; adrenalin seeping though our veins and carrying us back up on stage.

As I take to my drum throne and adjust the mic, I glance at some movement off stage. And there in the wings, amongst the unused instruments and the discarded hoodies and left over wiring, is Ziggy and Sam, and more importantly, MY DAD.

All There Is
Simple Truths: Daisy Meadows

I tap my sticks. Dylan picks up my beat, and together
we play our song for Dad.

Half a lifetime torn away
And I'm breaking more with every day
I've had good times, and bad times
And I wish I had the key
To turn back time and find that piece of me

This moment, is all that there is,
It's all there ever will be
And I'm gonna grab it now to find that piece of me

It's time to roll up my sleeves, before it's too late
Do things I wanna do, be the chooser of my fate
Let the past go and make music in the rain
I'm releasing the future, getting free of the pain

Let loose the tornados, see clouds disappear
Exist, but now, no more living in fear
Living each day, not living on wishes
Bring on the sunshine and let me know what bliss is
Because this is the moment, It's all that there is
It's all there ever will be
And I'm gonna grab it now to find that piece of me

Thanks

When you first set out to write a book, you think it's going to be a solitary journey, but you soon discover it's not.

There are many people who have contributed both to my development as a writer, and to Bring Me Sunshine, and I would like to say thank you to all of you, for your help and support on this journey. You are too numerous to mention everyone by name, but please know that I value and appreciate the time and feedback you have kindly given to me.

Especial thanks to Kate, for being my Applecore partner and for holding my hand through the publication maze; to Steve Parkman and Graham Robinson for their help with the cover and to Dave for the lyrics.
Thank you to Heather, Dave, and Lauren for the inspiration to create something meaningful, and for filling my life with music.
Thank you, Alan, for everything.

And finally, thank you to the carers, young and old; you make the world a better place.

Printed in July 2019
by Rotomail Italia S.p.A., Vignate (MI) - Italy